CROSSING THE LINE

SYLVIA GUNNERY

Cover by
Neil MacLachlan

Originally published as
We're Friends, Aren't We?

Scholastic Canada Ltd.

For my parents

Scholastic Canada Ltd.
175 Hillmount Road, Markham, Ontario, Canada L6C 1Z7

Scholastic Inc.
555 Broadway, New York, NY 10012, USA

Scholastic Australia Pty Limited
PO Box 579, Gosford, NSW 2250, Australia

Scholastic New Zealand Ltd.
Private Bag 94407, Greenmount, Auckland, New Zealand

Scholastic Ltd.
Villiers House, Clarendon Avenue, Leamington Spa,
Warwickshire CV32 5PR, UK

Canadian Cataloguing in Publication Data

Gunnery, Sylvia
Crossing the line

Previously published under title: We're friends, aren't we?
ISBN 0-590-03850-8

I. Title.   II: Title: We're friends, aren't we?

PS8563.U575W47 1998   jC813'.54   C98-931139-2
PZ7.G86Cr 1998

5 4 3 2 1   Printed in Canada   8 9/9 0 1 2/0

June 27

A seagull swooped high above the Honda as Woody leaned into the dip of the curve and revved the bike to accelerate up the hill. He was feeling good, the kind of good that comes from getting to the other side — well, almost — of all the downers.

His red bow tie, tucked under the chin strap of the purple helmet, almost glowed. His tuxedo flapped out behind him like dramatic black wings. And his shoes, polished only hours before when he'd gotten ready to take Sonia to the graduation dance, had a scuff or two now marring the shine. He could feel grains of sand settling under his socks inside the shoes and thought about stopping to empty them out.

Sunshine gleamed with the first burst of morning in the clear, summery sky. Cass's bike was great. The smell of the salty, cool air still damp from nighttime was great. For Woody, right now, there wasn't much in the entire world that wasn't great, or at least on the way to perfection.

The tandem truck was winding its way slowly back from an all-nighter that took it from Montreal to this spot on the coast just three kilometres from home. Its driver, leaning back in his seat, comfortable behind the wheel, was planning breakfast: ham, two eggs over easy, lots of fresh coffee and a slice, or maybe three, of homemade bread toasted golden brown. Everything around him was familiar, a road he'd driven on a hundred times, and a thousand more if you counted the days he'd pedalled his way up the steep hills and sudden bends and dips when he was a kid. He yawned, placing the back of his large hand against his mouth.

Woody checked the gas gauge and decided he'd put a couple of bucks into Cass's tank at the all-night garage just past Frankie's Arcade. Cass wouldn't expect him to, but Woody appreciated the loan of the bike. It had cheered him up after the downer of the graduation dance.

The five sets of tires on the truck muttered along the narrow seaside road, curling around the corners, obedient to the manoeuvring of the steering wheel. The driver shrugged his stiff shoulders and tilted his head to one side, then to the other, to work out the kink that always marked the end of an all-nighter. When he'd dropped his partner off, back about five kilometres, he'd joked about being home soon where he could get some liniment, with no one to complain about the reek of wintergreen.

The driver yawned again, then leaned to wind

down the window. A bit of fresh morning air would clear away his drowsiness.

Woody wriggled his shoe against the footrest, trying to rearrange the uncomfortable pocket of sand. Just over this hill, he promised himself, he'd stop and empty the stuff out. He eased the bike toward the double yellow lines to avoid a scattering of loose gravel on the highway.

The truck got to the crest of the hill, where the road dipped sharply toward the rocky beach. The driver was still winding down the window with his left hand as his right hand began to pull the wheel to make the turn. A refreshing gust of air blew into the cab of the truck.

Suddenly, inexplicably, he saw a red bow tie and a purple helmet. In that frozen instant his eyes recorded the details in front of him — a bike, gleaming blue and silver and driven by a kid wearing a tuxedo, was at the edge of the double yellow lines. He didn't even have time to raise his left hand back to the steering wheel.

May 8

Woody closed the door of the career counsellor's office behind him and stood with a frown of indecision on his face. In front of him was an empty hallway lined with lockers. At the far end a janitor manoeuvred his wide, flat mop in the silence which would, in exactly six and a half minutes, be shocked out of existence by the blaring noonhour bell and the stampeding stream of people escaping from classrooms.

Decisions have to start somewhere, thought Woody to himself. He reached into the pocket of his denim jacket, pulled out the half-full pack of cigarettes and dropped them into the garbage can next to the counsellor's door.

Before he had taken even two steps away, doubts mocked him. Maybe it was a bit drastic to throw away a half-deck of smokes. He could quit after they were gone, or after graduation, or even wait until he got into medical school, if he ever really got there. Even if he did, that was at least

4

three years away. Three years in which, at the rate he was going now, he could smoke — what? Two packs every three days, twenty-five in a pack times three hundred and sixty-five days in a year — that would work out to about six thousand lung-filling, gratifying, relaxing, tongue-teasing smokes.

But how could he reach into the garbage can and yank them out now? It'd be just his luck that someone would come along, appearing out of nowhere, and watch him, his hand extended into the garbage, retrieving the pack. That would do less for his image than even the thick glasses that had hung on his nose ever since he was eight. If he got desperate, he decided, he could buy just one more pack.

Briefly he considered whether or not they'd come out with extra-extra-mild cigarettes for people like him whose careers forced them into worrying about their public image, people like doctors. Or maybe they'd invent ones with little bags provided to catch all the air-polluting smoke so he could have a quick drag or two between patients. A bit far-fetched, but so was taking tourist snaps of Mars, and look what they did with that.

Just as he reached the cafeteria, the bell rang. Maybe lunch would take his mind off — he took a deep, smokeless breath — the habit.

"Hey, Woody, going to the meeting?" Placing her tray beside his and sitting down with a flourish of organising some notepapers and her lunch, Elizabeth Douglass smiled at him with her sea-blue eyes.

Cass's Elizabeth.

Woody had long ago given up any hope that she would ever be more than a friend, since grade five when she'd asked him to her birthday party and he was the only boy invited. That had sent him for a loop — until he got to the party. Not that she was trying to say he was a girl or anything like that, but it became obvious that she thought of him the same way she thought of the girls in their class. Good ol' Woody, good ol' friend-who'd-never-be-a-boyfriend Woody. That had been hard to take. But he'd made up for it by keeping his mouth shut around the guys so they'd think he had a big secret about what had gone on at the party. That lasted for about four days. It had been worth it.

"Sure I'm going. Didn't I say I'd go?" he replied.

"Hey, don't bite my head off."

"I just said I was going to the meeting. And I'm going. Simple. I'm not biting anybody's head off."

"Okay, okay. And listen, Woody, we need more guys there. I mean, it's their graduation too. We can't do it all. And besides, they'll say we took over everything and didn't let them have a word on the decorations or the band and stuff."

"Mark said he'd come."

"Good. He can draw. That'll be a big thing — the drawing."

"But he said if all he was doing was painting hearts all over graduation caps he'd quit."

"No problem."

"Hi, Woody. Elizabeth." Sliding his lunch tray down opposite Woody's, Paul straddled his chair as if he was riding a horse. "What's new?"

"Nothing."

"Hey," said Paul, "saw you and Cass this morning, Elizabeth. He brought you to school on his bike, didn't he?"

"Yeah."

"Thought you weren't allowed to see him. Thought that trouble he got in last weekend really fixed it."

"So much for thought."

"Now who's biting off heads?" said Woody.

"Well, everyone's going around saying stuff they don't know anything about. It's getting to me. It's getting to Cass."

"Wait a minute. You were the one who told me you couldn't see him. I didn't start that." Paul hunched his shoulders over the french fries he'd covered with ketchup.

"Look, I figure someone with a big mouth" — she gave Paul a look that measured the size of his mouth — "might tell Mom and Dad they saw me with Cass and I'll be grounded again. They won't listen to me or Cass. Dad just about had a fit when Cass showed up to talk to him. He wouldn't give him a chance to even start."

"Well, I hate to say anything to back up your parents," said Woody, adjusting his glasses on his nose, "but he did get things stirred up last Saturday night — or should I say Sunday morning? Using the soccer field as a stunt field isn't exactly bright."

"But he was drinking," said Elizabeth, exasperated.

"Oh, fine. That makes it all okay, of course. Just calmly sit across the dinner table and put on your sweetest daughter smile and say, 'Dearest Daddy, Cass, the love of my life, didn't mean to burn around the soccer field at two in the morning on Sunday. He was just wasted out of his little skull, that's all . . . ' "

"I know, Woody, I know. It's a mess. But he never drinks or shows off like that when we're together."

"Maybe you can get your dad to let him move into your house so he'll always be on his best behaviour."

"Cut it out, Woody. I'm serious."

Paul pushed his empty tray aside and leaned back in his chair. "What about graduation?"

"What about it?" asked Woody. Lately he was growing more and more paranoid at the mention of that word. He didn't have a date yet and that was information he wanted to keep to himself.

"I mean for you, Elizabeth. What about the dance? If your folks won't let you hang around with Cass — "

She wouldn't let him finish. "Cass will be taking me to the dance. It's more than a month away. Dad and Mom'll be cooled down by then."

"But what if they're not?"

"They will be." She got up, sifted through her notes and picked up her lunch tray. "Look, I gotta get to that meeting. Remember you said you'd be there, Woody. If you change your mind, Paul . . . "

"Nah. Drawing and stuff's not for me. I'm on clean-up."

"Sure. Okay. See you in three minutes, Woody. Bye, Paul."

When Elizabeth was out of hearing, Paul leaned across the table, almost secretly. "That girl is in for an eye-opener."

"What d'ya mean?" Woody didn't like being in the middle when someone started in about someone else.

"I mean Cass. They won't change their minds about him before graduation."

Woody drained the last of the milk in the small container. Elizabeth's parents were super strict. Always had been. Fifteen might not be twenty, but it wasn't twelve either. Still, the last thing he wanted now was to talk to Paul about it. He might as well tell the daily newspaper.

"She'll have to get tickets soon," continued Paul.

"She'll get the tickets."

"Yeah, but what if they still say no about Cass?"

"She'll figure out something."

"She hasn't got much time."

"Not that it's any of my business, but what's in it for you, Paul? You gonna ask her to go with you instead?"

"Thought about it."

"Forget it."

"Maybe not."

"Forget it. She'll work something out and she'll be there with Cass."

"Maybe. Let's go out for a smoke, Woody. You got time?"

"Sure," said Woody automatically. Then, touching the empty denim pocket, he pictured the half-smoked pack smothered in the garbage can under flunked tests and apple cores. "Ah — maybe I'd better get to that meeting. I'd just get out there and have to come right back in."

"Up to you. See ya later."

"Sure."

"Hey, Woody! Have you seen Elizabeth?"

It was Tony Cassidy — Cass — sitting across his Honda 750 holding his silver and red helmet in his hands.

"Oh, hi, Cass. What's up? How'd you get over here so fast?"

"Some sort of staff meeting. They let us out early. Have you seen Elizabeth?"

"Yeah. I mean no. I saw her at noon at the graduation meeting but not after that. She'll be out soon."

"Sure." Cass settled back on the leather seat of the bike, closely watching everyone who came down the high school steps. A lot of the girls checked him out as they walked by.

"Bricked up any classroom doors lately?" teased Woody.

Cass laughed. "No, but some kids said they're going to get this one teacher on the last day of school. Geez, I'd love to be there. He'll open the door and bam! — a brick wall staring him in the face."

"You guys have fun over there. Not like here."

"Community college is different."

"Yeah."

10

"Hey, Woody, Elizabeth said anything about the graduation dance? About tickets?"

"Yeah. She said you're going to take her. She said her folks'd forget all about everything by then. Why?"

"I dunno. It's pretty bad this time, I think. What do you think?"

"I dunno. I'll tell you this for sure. Elizabeth's going to that dance with you or she won't go at all. I could guarantee it."

"Her father won't even talk to me."

"What if someone tells about you driving her to school or being here now?"

"Who'll tell?"

"Just what if?"

"It won't happen. Besides, we don't go near her place. I meet her at Carolyn's and take her back there. God, do you believe her parents!" Cass ran his fingers through the long strands of dark hair that fell across his forehead.

"Hey, there she is." He grinned, waving at Elizabeth as she walked down the school steps.

In her new jeans, her straight, long brown hair caught up lightly by the wind, she had all the grace of a dancer, Woody thought. Cass was lucky.

"Cass! What're you doing here? Are you cutting class?"

He frowned. "Now that's a great welcome."

"I only meant — "

"I know. Ready for a ride?"

"Ready! Here, take these for me, will you, Woody?" said Elizabeth, passing her books to him and swinging her leg across the back of Cass's bike. She slid an old, battered helmet over her silken hair. "I'll get them later at your place. If you see Mom, just say I had a meeting or something."

"I'm not saying anything, Elizabeth. I'm not saying I saw you and I'm not saying I didn't. But if you want my advice — "

"Save it, Woody. We're friends, aren't we?"

Woody shrugged.

"Where to?" asked Cass, standing up to start the bike.

"Just around. Then to Carolyn's."

With a roar they left Woody at the curb, still holding too many books even after he'd stuffed most of them in his backpack.

But there was no time to think about Elizabeth's problem. Woody wanted a smoke and he had none — though his hands were too full to hold one even if he did. His lungs were beginning to get weak. He was sure his brain wasn't equipped to handle the absence of nicotine.

Then he saw Paul. "Hey, Paul! Wait up!"

"Got a bit of homework, eh, Woody?" Paul said with a smirk.

"Most of these are Elizabeth's. She went for a ride with Cass."

"Cass? How come he was here?"

"Dunno." Woody didn't want to supply Paul's megaphone mouth with information.

"That girl's losing it. She's gonna get grounded for sure."

"She'll do all right. Got a smoke? I'm out."

"No. So am I."

Woody slumped.

"Where you going now?" asked Paul.

"Home. With these. Before they deform my arms."

"You asked anyone to graduation yet?"

"Nah. Haven't made up my mind," said Woody flatly.

"Who's on the list?"

"Elizabeth's not, that's for sure."

"What's that supposed to mean?"

"Whatever you want it to mean."

"Meaning I shouldn't ask her."

"If you want to waste your breath, that's your business."

"What's with you, Woody? You get a couple of rejections already?"

"I didn't ask anyone yet."

"Geez, you're touchy."

"I guess. Look, Paul, these books are going through a transformation from paper to cement. Gotta go."

"Sure. See ya tomorrow."

Smoke. Smoke. Smoke. Inhale. Inhale. Hold it. Fill out those lungs. Exhale. Paradise! The rhythm of his steps along the sidewalk provided Woody's fantasy smoking with a beat. The beat was just as boring as the naked air that filled his lungs. By the time he was walking up his front steps, balancing the load of books and searching his pocket for the house key, Woody was in an undeniably bad mood.

And it wasn't just the smokes. He didn't have the vaguest idea who he'd ask to the graduation dance.

The load shifted its centre of gravity and the books tumbled into ruins on the mat at his feet. He stood looking at them, trying to decide whether he should count to ten or smash his fist into the door. Then he dismissed both ideas in favour of a few muttered exclamations as he picked up the books.

It was about quarter to five. His parents weren't home from work yet and Woody was lying on his back on the living room floor with a mind-filling blare of heavy metal blasting into his earphones. Oblivion!

Suddenly he sat up and grabbed the earphones off his head. He'd seen — nah, couldn't be. He thought he'd seen a head of hair bob up at the window. He stared.

There it was again! And this time it had eyes, blue ones, and a voice. "Woody!"

"Elizabeth?"

He rushed to the door and opened it. She made her way out of the juniper bushes.

"You deaf? I've been ringing the bell and pounding on the door."

"Listening to some CDs."

"I came for my books."

"Got some time? Come on in."

"Sure. What's up?"

"Nothing. Want a Coke or juice or something?"

"Juice. Got any food?"

"Let's look."

In the kitchen they tore at a leftover turkey.

"Elizabeth, I think someone else might be asking you to graduation."

"Who? What for?"

"Can't say who. But he thinks you're not going to be allowed to go with Cass."

"I will." She picked at the turkey leg, almost absent-mindedly, not at all interested in who the guy might be.

"I don't know who to ask," said Woody simply. For the second time in one day he was tossing that information out like it was no big deal.

"There must be somebody you like."

"Lots of people."

"Make a list and start at the top."

"I think I'd get to the bottom in one day of rejections."

"Don't be silly, Woody. Lots of girls would like to go with you."

"Name three."

"Ahh — well — "

"See."

"Give me a minute! There's Janet."

"David asked her."

"David!"

"Yeah."

"Hmmm. Well, how about Annmarie Boyd?"

"She's a bit young, don't you think?"

"Lots of women like older men."

"Then I'll wait until she's a woman."

"Come on, Woody. You know lots of girls."

"Sure. But I've never taken any out. I've just gone to parties and places with the rest of the gang. Even that time you and Hyram Jacobs and Beverly Weston and I went to the show when we were in grade seven I didn't really ask her. Hyram asked you and you asked Beverly and me to go too because you wouldn't go with him by yourself. You can't call that a date."

"Oh, God, Woody. Remember that? It kills me to think of it. Hyram stretching all out of shape to put his arm around me. He was so short."

"Still is."

"But, Woody, there's got to be somebody. I mean, this is graduation. You can't go alone and you have to go, so you have to have a date."

"Yeah. Sounds logical. But — "

"Look, I gotta get home or Mom'll be calling Carolyn and then she'll start pacing. Tell you what. I'll rack my brains tonight. Tomorrow we'll have someone all figured out."

"Sure," said Woody.

When the phone rang a few minutes later he figured it was Elizabeth looking for an excuse about where she'd been. But it wasn't. Carolyn was on the other end of the line.

"Did you know it's Elizabeth's birthday next weekend? I'm having a party for her. A surprise."

Woody perked up. That's just what he needed — a good chance to party. "I'll be there. Who's going?"

"Everybody."

"Cass?"

"Mom and Dad said no. I've already asked them.

Elizabeth's parents talked to them about Cass. Mom says she thinks they're treating Elizabeth like a little kid, but it's none of our business."

"So are there going to be birthday presents at this party?" he asked, to change the subject.

"Up to you."

"I know this CD she'd like."

"Good. Listen, I want everyone here by eight o'clock. She's coming over about eight-thirty. She thinks we're going to watch a movie and work on the chemistry questions for our project."

"Are you telling Cass about the party?" he asked.

"I don't know. What do you think? Should I?"

"Maybe. I mean, it is her birthday."

"But then I'll have to say he can't come. Her parents would have a fit if he showed up."

"He knows where things stand."

"Okay. I'll phone him. I feel stupid, but I think you're right. At least he'll know."

Upstairs in his room Woody stood in front of his bureau and stared into the mirror. He did have the look of a doctor — serious and a bit pale, and those bottle-thick glasses gave him an air of intelligence. He took off the glasses. He leaned close to the mirror to study his naked face and then took a step backwards. In front of him the image in the mirror blurred to a ghostly quiver of grey. He leaned forward again. The ghost turned into a blunt close-up of his plain face with a few spokes of hair under his nose — the five hairs that forced him into shaving every morning so no one would get on his case about trying to hide his top lip or some other stupid exaggeration like that. It wasn't a bad face really.

He looked at the shadows in the mirror. Gazing around his room, he noted the hulking shape of his bed and the posters on the wall beside it. He vaguely saw the desk and bookshelves, and the bright red blur of his skis and ski boots standing in the corner. Things didn't look real, he thought, but at least he could tell what they were. Maybe he could try winging it without his glasses. Maybe at Carolyn's party.

The next morning Elizabeth was half a block ahead of Woody when he left for school. By the time he caught up with her his lungs were pushing hard, gasping for air. Maybe it would take years before they got back in shape, he thought, pressing his hand against his wheezing chest.

"Oh good, it's you, Woody. I figured out who you should take to graduation. Belinda."

"Belinda? You mean Carolyn's sister?"

"Yeah. She's only a year behind us and she's probably hoping someone will ask her to graduation. What d'you think?"

"Hmm. I'll have to give that some consideration. Never thought of her. Isn't she going with someone?" It seemed to him that a girl that beautiful must be going with someone.

"No."

"Hmmm." His mind was already busy showing memory photos of her. Just yesterday he'd seen her in the hall by the gym door. She'd been wearing her gym gear — blue shorts and a white T-shirt with her name on the back. Those long, creamy brown legs . . .

"She's nice too," Elizabeth added.

Although he couldn't mention this to Elizabeth, her surprise birthday party might be the perfect place to ask Belinda. Things were beginning to fall into place.

May 18

Woody decided to wear his glasses for the walk to Carolyn's party — safer, because she lived three blocks away and there were bound to be obstacles like kids' bikes overturned and ready to grab his ankles and throw him flying, or like curbs that dropped one step before he expected.

As soon as he rang Carolyn's doorbell he tucked the glasses into his backpack.

"Woody?"

"Who d'you think it is?"

"You smash your glasses or something?"

He hadn't thought about how he'd explain why he was going around with a bare face.

"Not smashed, just out of commission."

"C'mon in," said Carolyn, holding the door open.

He tripped on the welcome mat and stifled a mutter when Carolyn's mother smiled at him from the living room sofa.

"Mom, this is Woody Harris. He usually wears glasses."

"But they're no big deal," he added.

"Let's go downstairs. A lot of people are here already. Want me to take your hand or something?"

"How about a white cane? Or do you happen to have a seeing-eye dog around?"

"Just trying to help."

A thudding rhythm could be heard seeping from the rec room, and when Carolyn opened the door music blared loudly up the stairs with a rush of warm air.

Woody cautiously reached to touch the wall for security and started down the steps behind Carolyn.

The rec room was a vague melting of reds and blues. She must've switched the regular bulbs with coloured ones, he thought. No one was dancing. There were small clumps of people standing along the wall by the stereo and sitting on the large L-shaped sofa in front of the fireplace. There were only a few quiet flames of fire, just for effect.

Carolyn had on a blue sweater with something that glittered as the red and blue lights splashed on it. All the faces were a blur of white or brown. Woody could barely see who was in front of him in the dimly lit room. And he had an even weirder feeling that no one could clearly see him standing there.

"Hey, Woody, where's your goggles?"

It was Paul's voice, and as it came nearer, his face emerged from the dimness.

"Just not wearing them."

"Why not?"

"No reason. Didn't feel like it."

"Well, let me know if you want anything translated into vision for you. For instance, you are now standing in Carolyn's rec room."

"Stifle it, Paul."

"What's that?"

"What's what?" asked Woody, turning his head this way and that.

"Under your arm."

"Oh. Elizabeth's present. Where's Carolyn gone? I forgot to give this to her."

"Over by the fireplace. That's due west about sixty-eight degrees and north seven."

"Funny. Remind me to laugh."

Woody cracked his knee against a low table that crouched at the end of the sofa.

"Here's Elizabeth's present, Carolyn. Where should I put it?" he asked, rubbing his screaming knee.

"Over by the birthday throne."

"Huh?"

"Oh, I forgot. Come with me." She took Woody's hand and dragged him over to a chair which was decorated to look like a throne. "This is where she'll sit to open her presents."

"Many people bring presents?"

"Sure. Even Paul."

"Paul?"

"Yeah."

"You're telling me that Paul brought Elizabeth a birthday present?"

"Why not? You did."

"Yeah, but — oh, never mind." He watched her place his gift beside the chair in the pile of bows and colourfully wrapped boxes.

There were more things to think about than Paul's idea of cutting in on Cass. For one thing, seeing. Then, of course, there was asking Belinda to graduation.

He strained to see what he was looking at. It's funny how, when you can't, you want to see even boring things like blue lights in table lamps, Woody thought. And there was the immediate problem of trying to find Belinda. He figured she must be at the party, but so far he couldn't tell for sure.

"Hey, Carolyn, is Belinda coming?"

"She's over there. Boy, you do need glasses."

Sauntering over, Woody cased the situation as it came into focus. Paul and a couple of girls were there, so he wouldn't have to say anything to Belinda right away.

She was taller than Carolyn, he noticed, standing next to her. And she had on perfume, not the sick kind that makes your nose suffocate, but a kind that smelled like mild soap. Her sweater was red with something white on it, but he couldn't quite see what it was.

"Elizabeth's coming!" announced Carolyn in a whispered shout. "Turn off the player. Get the lights. Shhhhh!"

She rushed up the stairs, shutting the door quietly.

"Shhhh."

Everyone squashed in a pile under the staircase.

Woody was crammed in beside Belinda, enjoying it. The white something on her sweater, he could distinguish now, was a little flower brooch, like a daisy or something. Cute. Maybe a bit youngish but still cute. Maybe, right now, anything Belinda wore would be cute.

They could hear Carolyn telling Elizabeth about working on the chemistry project downstairs. She said something about the fireplace. She was saying it so loud it was a wonder she didn't give the whole surprise away.

Then the door opened and the two girls started down the stairs.

"I must've left the lights off. Stupid me."

"I'll get the one at the top here," offered Elizabeth.

"No, it's all right, I'll just — "

The lights clicked on, blue and red, and the mob under the stairs tumbled out with yells of "Surprise! Surprise!" and "Happy Birthday!"

"Oh, my God," moaned Elizabeth, covering her face with her hands.

"Hey, Elizabeth! Open the presents!"

"Oh, my God," she muttered again, looking up, her face shining red. Maybe there were even tears in her eyes. Woody couldn't tell.

Everyone belted out a questionable version of "Happy Birthday to You" and Elizabeth cautiously sat on the birthday throne. Belinda picked up a present and handed it to her. She read the card out loud. "Birthdays look good on you. Happy birthday from Paul."

Some ooh's went up from the crowd but Paul didn't say anything.

"A necklace. It's beautiful," said Elizabeth. "Thank you."

Woody could tell from her voice that she was embarrassed. It wasn't long before he knew exactly why.

"What's with the heart, Paul?" said one of the guys. "You and Elizabeth got some secret we don't know?"

"Wait'll Cass finds out," joked a different voice.

"Open another present, Elizabeth," said Carolyn, coming to the rescue.

And the fuss about the heart-shaped necklace died down. Woody figured, though, that Elizabeth's mind was buzzing with thoughts about Cass and about Paul. She'd probably figured out that Paul was the guy Woody had been referring to when he'd told her that someone else was planning to ask her to graduation.

After the gifts were opened, the music was turned up until the walls were bouncing with sound. Woody found Belinda and asked her to dance. She looked terrific moving with the beat and singing all the words to the song. But then again, he daydreamed, she'd look great standing like a block of bored cement. He decided not to ask her to the grad dance until at least three more songs, and one of them would have to be a slow number.

But when the slow number came on, Elizabeth was immediately at Woody's side, dragging him to the centre of the room.

"Save my life, Woody," she muttered as she wrapped her arms around him.

"Wha— "

"Paul's the one, isn't he?"

"One? Wha— "

"Don't pretend you don't know, Woody. He's been staring at me all night. And that necklace — he is, isn't he?"

"Yeah."

"He knows I'm going with Cass. He knows I don't like him that way. What's he trying to prove?"

"Look, Elizabeth, Paul's just trying to say he likes you. Lots of guys like you. All you have to do is say no. What's the big deal?"

"It just bugs me, that's all."

Over Elizabeth's shoulder, Woody squinted into the dark to find Belinda. Under the staircase he thought he saw a blur of red mixed in with a blur of grey and he guessed it was Belinda and someone. They didn't look like they were dancing.

"Did you ask her yet?"

"Huh?"

"Belinda."

"Didn't get a chance."

"Better move fast. She looks a bit involved with Glenn right now."

Woody pretended he could see what they were doing. His imagination filled in the details.

Carolyn's mother came downstairs and made her way over to Elizabeth. Couples untangled as the dance ended.

"You have a visitor, Elizabeth. I'm not sure your

parents would approve, but it is your birthday and he wants to give you a gift. I guess there's no harm in that."

"Cass?" said Elizabeth.

Wherever Paul was, thought Woody, he should see the look on Elizabeth's face now. You could tell she was really glad — and surprised.

When Elizabeth got to the living room Carolyn's father was standing next to Cass, who had a gigantic box in his arms. It was wrapped in shiny gold paper with a royal blue bow on top.

"Happy birthday," he said.

It was awkward. What are you supposed to do when you're standing there with two parents — practically strangers — staring at you? thought Elizabeth.

By some miracle of understanding, Carolyn's mother took her husband by the hand and led him into the kitchen.

"How's your surprise party?" asked Cass.

"Really great. I mean — it's fun and all, but . . . "

"What?"

"It would be better if you were here."

"I'm here." He grinned and placed the huge gift in her arms. "Open this."

Carolyn's parents came out of the kitchen and went downstairs with trays of pizza hot out of the oven.

Carefully Elizabeth tugged at the ribbon that held the bow, and then peeled back the strips of tape. She planned to save everything — the bow, the paper and especially the gift, no matter what it was.

"I can't even guess what this is."

"I might've done a dumb thing — you know, with your parents thinking the way they're thinking right now."

Finally she lifted the top from the box and pulled out wads of tissue paper to reveal a metallic purple bike helmet. In small gold lettering on the sides were her initials — *E.M.D.*

"Oh, Cass, it's the best. It's the very best!" She held him and the purple helmet in one cluttered hug. Then she slid the helmet on and fastened it under her chin.

Cass stared at her as if she were wearing a crown.

"Let's try it out!" she said in a rush of excitement.

"What d'you mean?"

"Just around the block. Everyone's downstairs. Who'll know? No one!"

"Let's go!" Cass grabbed her hand and they started for the door.

"Wait! My jacket!" Laughing, she stopped at the hallway closet.

Then they were out the door and running down the driveway. Behind them noises from the party boomed out through a lower window.

"What d'you think Cass got Elizabeth?" Carolyn asked Woody.

"Dunno." He was trying to figure out which pizza had onions. He hated onions.

"He's neat," said Carolyn, helping herself to a

second piece of pizza with stringy cheese and lots of mushrooms.

"But it isn't going to work." Woody sniffed cautiously for onions. "I was thinking about that a while ago. Cass won't slow down or cool down or whatever you want to call it. She's a kid compared to him. They're too different." Woody squinted at what he hoped wasn't an onion on the edge of his slice of pizza.

"But he loves her."

"Yeah."

"You don't think so, do you?"

"Looks something like love. But I dunno. He's nineteen. She's fifteen — sixteen," he corrected himself. "And he's been around a lot more than she has."

"You sound like her father."

"Mmm," he muttered through a delicious mouthful.

"Carolyn, come here, please," her mother called from the stairway. "Right away."

Woody walked over to see what was up because he was sure it had to do with Elizabeth.

"What, Mom?"

"I'm afraid Elizabeth has left her party."

"What?"

"She's gone. With Cass. Just as your father and I were coming up the stairs we heard the motorcycle driving off. And her coat is gone. I want you to call her parents."

"Do we have to stop the party?"

"Of course not, but we must inform her parents."

"I'll come with you, Carolyn." Woody wished he

had his glasses on now that things were getting serious. He decided to retrieve them from his backpack.

"Where would she go?" asked Carolyn's mother.

"If you ask me," said Woody, adjusting his glasses on his nose, "they've just gone around the block and they'll be back before the Douglasses even answer their phone."

"Hello, Mrs. Douglass," said Carolyn with a frown in Woody's direction. "My mother wanted me to call you but I don't think it's a big deal and Woody doesn't either, but Cass came to the party to give Elizabeth a birthday present and then when we came upstairs they were both gone, but Woody says they've just gone around the block and we shouldn't think it's a big deal."

Funny how a long sentence can make something sound like a big deal, thought Woody.

"Well, I don't think you have to come over. Just a minute." She covered the receiver and frantically said to her mother, "They want to come over! Oh, Mom, talk them out of it, please. It'll ruin the party. Just tell them to wait a few minutes and we'll call them as soon as they get back."

Her mother took the phone and began to reassure Elizabeth's mother. It didn't seem to be working. Carolyn and Woody stared at each other as if somehow they could make Elizabeth zap back onto the scene by wishing hard.

It wasn't cold out at all, but Elizabeth felt a shiver of excitement as she clung to Cass's leather jacket.

With a turn of his right wrist, Cass accelerated. Strands of Elizabeth's hair had been tugged out from underneath the helmet by the wind and fluttered in small whipping motions against her face. She grinned with the thrill of wearing her own purple helmet. Cass's gift was perfect! Cass was perfect!

Hugging him, she could feel through his body the humming rhythm of the Honda 750 as he wound the accelerator up further. They turned onto the ramp leading to the highway. In moments they were speeding along in the darkness. Then, briefly, the high beams of an oncoming car captured them. She closed her eyes and held tighter, smelling the dull leather of Cass's jacket, mixed with the cool night air.

"How's the helmet?" Cass yelled back over his shoulder.

"Great! Great!" She hugged him even more. There was so much noise and wind that she felt as though they were in some strange land rather than on the short stretch of highway minutes from where she lived. The glare of traffic lights created a wall they could fly through and the wind lifted their shouts to where no one else could hear.

With a lean in unison, they moved out into the passing lane, then balanced to centre as the bike pulled ahead of a lazy car. Easily, safely, they slipped back into the right-hand lane as though drawn by a magical string. Cass's bike was solid and fast and he controlled it with the power of experience.

As the skyline of tall buildings, dotted with lights, receded farther and farther, Elizabeth had a dangerous feeling of freedom, almost of escape. It was as though Cass could keep the 750 pointed away from home forever. She wished it would stay dark like a black shelter around them. Somehow the wind had the power to scatter all the rules into meaningless, forgotten corners.

"I'm so happy, Cass!" she yelled against the rush of wind.

At the first exit he slowed the bike and turned onto the ramp to double back to Carolyn's. When the 750 finally muttered to a stop, both Elizabeth and Cass recognized her father's car parked at the end of the driveway.

"I'd better come in too," Cass said.

"Where have you been?" Her father's stern voice greeted them before they were even inside the door.

"Cass gave me this," Elizabeth said, holding the purple helmet in her hands, "and — well, I just wanted to try it out."

"We just did the loop around the first exit on the new highway, sir," offered Cass carefully.

"The point is, and it seems you've both forgotten, Elizabeth has been asked not to see you. You have to understand, whether it appears unreasonable or not, that her mother and I have discussed this and have made that decision final."

Elizabeth started to say something but then sighed, looking down at her own vague reflection in the smooth curve of the helmet.

"I'm sorry, sir. I guess I shouldn't have taken

her." Cass put his hand on the doorknob to leave and then turned to Elizabeth. "Well, happy birthday. I'll be seeing you. I mean — "

"Just a moment, Cass," said Mr. Douglass. "I know you will understand when I ask you to take your gift back."

"Dad!" protested Elizabeth. "You can't make me do that!"

"Please don't cause another scene, Elizabeth," said her mother. "If you're not to see Cass, and especially since your father and I don't want you to be driving on that motorcycle, then it's best to return Cass's gift. I'm sorry, dear, but that's final."

"It's okay, Elizabeth. I don't mind. You got to wear it, didn't you? And you looked terrific." He held out his hands for the helmet and she gave it to him.

If her parents had been in tune with things at all they might have been able to notice the brief exchange between Elizabeth and Cass. In one almost imperceptible glance they made an important plan for the helmet and Elizabeth smiled, knowing she'd get to wear it again.

"Good night, Mrs. Douglass, Mr. Douglass, 'Night, Elizabeth." He shut the door behind him.

"I want to go home too," Elizabeth said. "Wait so I can thank Carolyn." She went downstairs and everyone in the room watched her, expecting tears.

"We'll help you with your presents," offered Carolyn. "Come on, Woody."

As they gathered the ribbons and gifts together, Elizabeth remembered her suggestion that Woody ask Belinda to graduation. "Did you ask her?" she whispered.

"Yes. She said no," said Woody with a that's-just-the-way-it-goes look on his face.

"She's crazy."

"She's going steady with Glenn as of tonight."

"Oh. Well, back to the drawing board."

"What're you going to do?" he asked, putting one more gift on the pile.

"About what?"

"About graduation? It looks like for sure your folks are sticking to what they said."

"I'll be going with Cass," she stated confidently and turned to go up the stairs. "Thanks for the party everyone!"

In the back seat of her father's car Elizabeth slouched silently, holding her gifts on her lap.

"I guess you think we're terrible parents," said her mother in a quiet voice.

She had nothing to reply to that. The next line would probably be something like, "We're doing it for your own good."

"Your father and I are just worried that you're too young to be serious with one boy. When you're older you'll understand."

Silence again.

The night air rushed in through her father's open window and rustled the bows on top of the pile of gifts. The largest bow was the royal blue one that had been on Cass's present. She wondered what he was doing now. There was little chance she'd see him the next day because it was Sunday and because her parents would be extra nosy about where she went and what she did for a while. No chance of slipping away to see Cass tomorrow.

She continued to give the silent treatment, looking out at the quiet streets, staring with blank disinterest at the carefully mowed lawns. When the car stopped in their driveway she got out first and opened the front door with her own key, managing the gifts all by herself.

Her parents had taken the hint. They didn't stop her when she went directly to her room.

Woody had lost enthusiasm for the party. It wasn't the thing with Belinda either. She'd been nice about saying no. But it was hard to have a party for someone who'd left, not that he blamed Elizabeth.

"Wanna split?" Paul had obviously lost interest too.

"Sure. Soon's I talk to Carolyn."

Woody found her on the sofa, sat down beside her and half smiled.

"Some party," she said drearily. "I shouldn't have told Cass about it. She'd still be here if it wasn't for him."

"True. But if I know Elizabeth she's probably thinking the ride on his bike with her new helmet was worth all the trouble. This'll blow over."

"I'm not so sure."

"Great party though."

"Mmm," she responded unenthusiastically.

"I mean it. It was!"

"Was."

"Paul and I are heading out. Give Elizabeth a call tomorrow. You'll see. She'll say it was the best birthday she ever had, thanks to you."

"Sure."

"She will. I had a great time too. I really did. Even if your misguided kid sister decided to pick tonight to fall in love with Glenn and refused my invitation to the graduation."

"You asked Belinda?" Carolyn brightened, with a sly grin on her face. "Woody, you didn't!"

"Sure I did. It was Elizabeth's idea but I thought it was a good one. I'm sorry she said no."

"You and Belinda? I can't believe it."

"What's to believe? I only asked her to graduation. I wasn't planning to empty my bank account for a diamond ring, you know."

"My kid sister and you?" She fell back against the sofa cushions and laughed.

"Time to disappear," said Woody. "I wish I hadn't told you."

But he wasn't really bothered. Carolyn was cheered up now.

"It's bad enough having you around all the time at school without having you hanging around the house with Belinda," she teased.

"If her family wasn't such a drag I might try to cut in on Glenn."

"Cute, Woody. Cute."

"See you around."

"Yeah. And thanks."

"For what?" asked Woody.

"For the laugh."

Outside, Woody automatically reached into his backpack for cigarettes, but found only his glasses case. "Got a smoke, Paul?"

"Sure."

Sliding the cigarette out of Paul's package, Woody began to get the guilts. It had been eleven days since he'd actually held a cigarette in his hand. Eleven whole days! Maybe he should just skip it, give it back to Paul. But when Paul reached over with the lighter glowing there was no turning back. The first drag was a huge gulp, which he pulled deeply into his lungs. Instantly he started to cough. And cough.

"What happened?" asked Paul. He sounded as if he thought Woody was going to pass out right in front of him.

"Went down the wrong way," gasped Woody.

"That kind of thing happened to Mom when she was trying to quit," said Paul.

"Who said I'm trying to quit?"

"No one. It's just that I haven't seen you with a cigarette lately." Paul took a long drag and blew the smoke out in a laser line up into the air. "Listen, if you don't want that, butt it. I'll have it later."

"Nah. Think I'll smoke it."

"Up to you."

Silently they walked along, heading toward Frankie's Arcade. Woody tried to savour each puff of the cigarette, without much luck. It tasted guilty.

"Isn't that Cass's bike in front of Frankie's?" asked Paul.

It was Cass's Honda all right. The windshield curved up like a shell over the handlebars, and the custom paint job in metallic midnight blue with silver trim gleamed under the streetlight. On the gas tank was *HONDA* with an impressive gold wing flying off the name. There wasn't a splash of mud on the bike. Even the four exhaust pipes, like black cone trumpets, were spotless. You'd swear the guy never drove it, thought Woody. Not that he blamed Cass. The bike was an '81 and in mint condition.

Inside the arcade, games flashed and buzzed and hummed and zapped. Four or five guys hovered around each machine while one guy handled the controls and concentrated on winning.

"Hi, fellas," said Frankie from behind the cash register. "Can I sell you some change tonight?"

Woody bought some, but Paul was already on his way over to where Cass was racing a car on an animated race track that dipped and curved at dizzying speeds in front of him. His attention didn't waver for a second. Paul got caught in the action too, leaning his body almost automatically as Cass's car came into the hairpin turn. They both started back when, in a glaring yellow and orange flash, Cass's car exploded on impact with another one that had come up on the inside and spilled in front of him.

"That's the third time!" Cass said in frustration, hitting the side of the game.

"Let me try," said Woody.

He stood firmly in front of the game, his hands

on the controls, and took a deep breath. Then he put his money in.

At first cars began to move as if in slow motion. Then suddenly the track was moving at breakneck speed, signs and posts appearing and disappearing before they could really be noticed. Suddenly a turn! Woody manoeuvred his car through it. His hands gripped almost white on the controls as though at any minute his life could be ended in a smear of colour on the animated track. Fat wheels of other cars hemmed him in as they fought for the winning position, blues and reds and bright yellows challenging him. Another turn! A car instantly there on his right! Another ahead on the left! A squeeze! In a whir of alarm buzzes and the on-and-off glare of red and yellow lights, Woody wiped out.

"Not bad," said Cass slowly. "Almost caught up to my 68,490 mark."

"Put in more money," Paul said.

"What happened after I left?" asked Cass. "Elizabeth's parents seemed pretty mad."

"Yeah. They were. She went right home," replied Woody, fishing out some change. "She liked her helmet."

"I took it back to my place."

"Guess you got her in a pile of trouble with that helmet," said Paul, who, it seemed to Woody, was rubbing it in a bit much.

Cass didn't like it. "What's it to you?"

"Nothing," said Paul cautiously.

Cass kept staring at him as if he could read his

thoughts, and as if he didn't much like what he was reading.

"Listen, you guys," said Woody, "enough's happened tonight without you two starting a fight."

Paul looked a bit ruffled, but nervous.

Cass turned back to the game, seeming to dismiss the whole thing.

"You won't get to graduation for sure now," said Paul. He obviously didn't know thin ice when he was standing on it.

"Who says?" threatened Cass.

"Her parents."

"Could I butt in here again, you guys?" said Woody, stepping back from the game. "Look, Paul, you aren't in this deal at all. Even if you want to be. Cass, you might not get to graduation with Elizabeth. Admit it, things aren't looking good. And starting something up with Paul won't help anything."

He looked from one to the other.

"What are you, the law?" asked Cass.

Woody smiled but decided he'd said enough.

"Put some more money in," said Paul.

Woody fed a coin into the slot and focussed on the race that began to glow in front of him. In the instant before his concentration was swallowed up by the game, he decided he'd try to convince Paul, once and for all, that thinking he'd ever take Elizabeth to graduation was a dead-end street.

Elizabeth couldn't sleep. She turned over in her bed and looked across the room where the moon fell in a river of light across the birthday gifts piled on her chair. Cass's gift wasn't there but she could see it as clearly as if it were. It was the best gift he could have given her, she thought, feeling a rush of warmth for him. Then she pictured him leaving Carolyn's with the big box under his arm.

She turned on her light. Maybe reading would help.

A gentle tap sounded on her bedroom door. Since her light was on, she knew she couldn't pretend to be asleep. Might as well get it over with. Another heart-to-heart in which her mother would ask her to try to understand their point of view. If only *they'd* try to understand hers!

Another light knock. The doorknob began to turn slowly and she said, without enthusiasm, "I'm awake. Come in if you want."

But it was her father who stood in the doorway, his greying hair ruffled on the top, probably from running his hands through it a dozen times the way he always did when he was upset. "How's my little girl?"

"I'm not your little girl, Dad. I'm sixteen now. I'm just about to graduate." It bothered her that just by saying those words she sounded like a whining kid.

"I know, but when you're sixty-two, like I am, Bethy," he said with a smile, "being a little girl and being sixteen seem just about the same." He had slipped into using his nickname for her. A few years ago she'd asked him not to call her that and usually he didn't. Yet, standing in this room where she'd been a diapered baby, then a small child with knees constantly scabbed by falls, and where the porcelain teddy-bear lamp still glowed beside her bed, he couldn't think of her as grown up.

"But not for me, Dad. It's totally different!" Her heart ached with frustration. Over and over again they'd had the same conversation.

He sat on the edge of her bed and picked up the book she'd left open beside her. "What are you reading?"

"It's for school."

Looking up from the book, he said gently, "Your mother and I want you to be happy. You know that."

"It doesn't feel much like it."

"But we do all the same. You're the most important thing that's ever happened in our lives. We waited a long time before you came along and when you finally did — well, things were never the same."

Tears began to swell in Elizabeth's eyes. Her father looked so kind and almost timid sitting there in the dim light of her bedroom. You'd never think. he could be so angry and blow his top the way he sometimes did.

For some strange reason she thought of a time long ago when she was very little. She'd been sick in church and when they got home her mother had wrapped her in a blanket and laid her on the living room couch so she'd be close by. Her father had brought in some medicine. Chocolate stuff, he'd called it, as though that tantalising name could take away the ether reek or the chalky, bitter taste. When he'd forced a large spoonful into her mouth she'd choked. In a spray of chocolate colour the medicine had spewed all over her father's white shirt. Both he and Elizabeth had a quick moment of shock before the whole thing sank in.

She didn't remember much else — except that he hadn't been angry. He seemed to know that for her at that moment staying sick was infinitely better than the few brief seconds of cruel medicine.

"That boy may be nice in his way," her father went on now, "but he's too old for you and he's been in too much trouble. Your mother and I don't want you to be dragged into that. We just want to protect you. Even if it was your thirtieth birthday, we'd still feel the same."

"But surely when I'm thirty you won't expect me to live here and have you guys take care of me." She knew her voice was too loud but she couldn't help it. "You can't protect me forever. I'm more than halfway to thirty already, you know. I'll be going to university soon."

A resigned smile flashed on her father's face for an instant. He stared down at the cover of Elizabeth's book. "I wish you could understand," he said quietly.

"I wish *you* could understand!" she shot back.

He rested his hand for a moment on her arm and then stood up. "It's late. We're all tired. Maybe in the morning things will seem brighter." He left the room, shutting the door gently.

She stared at the clown puppet hanging from the

hook on the back of the door. Brighter in the morning, she thought with a scowl. He always said that, as though daylight could actually make things different. Tomorrow the helmet would still not be on the chair with the other gifts and Cass would still not be allowed to see her. Sweet sixteen! Ha! she thought bitterly. Might as well be six!

May 24

Friday afternoons were always the same — heightened excitement all around, kids laughing over nothing, beyond control because the end-of-Friday bell was only minutes away from ringing. Miss Johnston might be reading *Julius Caesar* out loud to the class, lamenting about *Et tu, Brute,* but not one other person in the entire room cared about whether or not Caesar got knocked off on the ides of March. It was Friday — loose and free Friday.

"Woody!"

He turned around from where he was rummaging through his locker, already recognising Elizabeth's voice.

"You going home?" she asked.

"Yeah."

"Me too."

Since noonhour, when Cass had come to school to visit her, the plan had been made. Only she needed Woody.

"Listen, I need a favour. Cass and I want to see

each other tonight. I haven't really had time with him since the party last Saturday."

"Where do I fit in?"

"I was just wondering if — well, if you weren't doing anything else maybe you'd come over to my place and say you were picking me up to go to a movie. Only I'd go see Cass and then we'd meet again and go back to my place as though we had really been to a movie."

"What if I say no?"

"Then I won't go. Simple."

"No."

"Aw, Woody."

"I knew it! You weren't even thinking I'd say no."

"I mean, if you're not doing anything — "

"Then I'm supposed to get in on your conspiracy."

"Come on. Be a friend."

"Look, Elizabeth, your parents don't want you to go out with Cass. I know they're strict but I can't do anything about that."

"It's just a couple of hours. You could go to a movie and then meet me after. Who'd know the difference?"

"Me."

"Aw, Woody."

"Aw, Elizabeth."

They were now at the end of their street.

"It was worth a try anyway," she said, defeated.

Something about the tone in her voice made Woody reconsider. Maybe her parents were overreacting. They usually did. Cass wasn't a bad guy.

"Well, I don't have anything better to do, I guess."

It took Elizabeth all of a microsecond to realize what he was saying. She hugged him right then and there, tilting his glasses precariously.

"What time do I pick you up and drop you off?"

"Well, we'd have to go by bus to the movie. So I guess if you got to my place by seven-thirty we could meet Cass at Frankie's and you could still go to a movie — if you want to, that is."

"Might as well. What movie am I seeing?"

She poked him in the ribs. "Don't tease."

"Just sounded like you had the whole thing worked out, that's all."

Luckily there actually was a movie he wanted to see. Horror. Blood. Screams in the night.

"Woody's here!" shouted Elizabeth's mother as she greeted him at the door when he arrived.

"Hi, Mrs. Douglass."

"Come in, Woody. You and Elizabeth haven't gone to a movie together for years, not since the Saturday matinees," she said. Then she added, "She wants to get out of the house for a change. I guess she feels we're being too strict."

He decided it was best not to get into that one.

"I'm glad you're going." She smiled weakly and tangled her knuckles together.

"Yeah." Woody thought of Pinocchio, whose nose grew and grew with every lie he told. Funny how a simple "yeah" could be a lie.

"I'm not sure she'll like this movie," he said, sitting up straighter on the sofa and then deciding that a slouch was the better choice. "Blood and guts."

"She won't care. She'll enjoy it."

"Yeah." He touched the end of his nose.

"We both think Tony Cassidy is nice in some ways, but — " She studied her hands. "She'll thank us when she's old enough to know these things."

"Hi, Woody. All set?" Elizabeth came into the room wearing a bright yellow sweatshirt with two streaks of red across the arms. Her eyes were full of excitement and her hair was so shiny it looked like it had been brushed for hours. Woody figured her mother would have to be blind not to see that it was Cass she was "all set" for.

"I've got an idea," said Mrs. Douglass. "Why don't you two come back here after the movie and we'll have pizza together? Brian'll be home then. We'll make it a foursome."

Elizabeth shot a glance at Woody which he couldn't easily translate. But the mention of pizza, especially the thick-with-cheese-and-oozing-with-homemade-sauce kind that Mrs. Douglass made, convinced Woody to hear only his own inner voice, which was now saying, "Food, food, food! Yes, yes, yes!"

"Great idea! We'll be back before midnight." Then, noticing an urgent look on Elizabeth's face he added, "If we can get the bus on time."

Elizabeth smiled, pleased with this loophole. He had the distinct feeling that his nose was growing.

The bus was just arriving at the stop outside the movie theatre as Woody emerged, so he'd be in lots of time getting back to Frankie's. He sat alone at the back, staring at his reflection in the window. He and Elizabeth had met Cass, as planned, in front of Frankie's. Cass had gripped Woody's shoulder saying, "Thanks, buddy," as if Woody had rescued Elizabeth from the jaws of a dragon.

"Yeah," Woody had said, promising himself that he wouldn't utter that noncommittal word once more that night.

But when he got back to Frankie's Cass and Elizabeth weren't there. And forty minutes later, at five after twelve, they still weren't there.

At twelve-twenty they finally pulled up in front, laughing as though it wasn't at all important that they were late. Woody was angry.

"Come on, Elizabeth. I told your mother we'd be back before midnight. We're late."

She looked at him as if he had two heads.

"What's the problem?" asked Cass.

"Look, I agreed to this. Right. But I don't want to make a scene with Elizabeth's parents. You know what they're like. I said I'd be back there half an hour ago and I'm not. I like to keep my word."

"Sure," said Cass. "Why don't I drive you two part way."

With a sigh Woody agreed. No sense bringing up the fact that the bike was meant for two people, not three, or that he didn't have a helmet. Might as well get this over with.

Cass stopped at the end of the street and let them off. Woody glanced up at nothing while Cass and Elizabeth said goodnight. Then he ran with her to her house.

"Say we missed the bus," whispered Elizabeth quickly as she opened the door with her key.

"There you are!" Mrs. Douglass greeted them. "The pizza's all ready."

"Hi, Mrs. Douglass, Mr. Douglass," Woody said awkwardly. "Sorry we're late."

"We missed the bus," said Elizabeth with a quick glance at Woody.

"That's what we thought," returned her mother, already halfway to the kitchen.

"How was the movie?" asked Mr. Douglass.

"Not bad."

"Great!" Elizabeth exclaimed at the same time.

"Did you both see the same movie?" laughed Mr. Douglass. "What was it called?"

Elizabeth looked at Woody with a plea in her eyes.

"*Winter Wolves of Fog Island Lake,*" he said without enthusiasm. "It had some good parts," he added, feeling like an impostor in front of Elizabeth's parents.

The pizza consumed, Woody got up from the sofa to head back home. They had managed to keep off the topic of the movie and that, at least, made him feel relaxed. Yet, deep inside, his thoughts were churning about what he'd done that night. It didn't feel right.

"I'll walk you part way over to your place," said Elizabeth as her mother and father cleared the dishes.

Outside, a few stars shone above the city lights. There was only the smallest breath of wind stirring the leaves that hung thickly on the large maple trees which lined the street.

"What a night!" Elizabeth said, inhaling the cool, fragrant air. She was obviously feeling pretty good about things.

"Yeah," Woody muttered.

"What's wrong?"

It occurred to him that he could avoid a scene by saying that nothing was wrong at all. What could possibly be wrong? But there had been enough lies told that night and he had to say what was on his mind.

"As long as nothing's wrong with you, nothing's wrong with anybody." He purposefully walked in long strides to make her hurry to keep up with him.

"You're mad about getting home late."

"Yes, I am. But it's a lot more than that." Woody stopped and looked directly at Elizabeth. "You know exactly what's bothering me. Don't play dumb."

"Look, Woody, I'm sorry I made you duck questions from Mom and Dad. I — "

"Sorry? Really? Or are you just happy you got to be with Cass tonight?"

"You could've said no," she said quietly.

"For a while there I thought you didn't even notice I was being dipped in acid to give you and Cass some time." He was not calming down at all. His anger seemed to bubble up with his words. "You know, Elizabeth, I've been sucked in. In a way

51

I deserve it. But they're your parents — you're stuck with them. And you're going to have to pull this kind of stunt on your own if you think it's the only way to handle the problem. Did you ever try talking to them about things?"

"Yes, I've tried, but they act like I'm a two-year-old. I'm their little girl who needs to be protected. What's the use?"

"Maybe you've got to show them they don't need to baby you all your life. Or maybe they're right — maybe you are a two-year-old!"

He turned to go.

"Woody! Wait!"

"Forget it!"

"Come on, Woody. What's the use of fighting? Come on. Have a heart!"

"Have a nightmare!"

But as he walked away he had a feeling that soon things would get really tense for Elizabeth. It was inevitable.

May 25

"Martha and Duncan are coming over this evening."

"So?"

"Is that any way to talk to your mother?" Putting down the magazine he'd been reading, Mr. Douglass stood up from his desk.

Elizabeth suppressed a childish urge to stick her tongue out at him. That morning she'd heard her mother talking too long and too quietly on the phone. Something was up. And since when did they have family gatherings on a Saturday night?

"All I meant was that I'm not really interested in Aunt Martha or in Duncan."

"Now that's not fair, Elizabeth. You've had great times when we've gone for holidays to their beach house. I thought you and Duncan were friends."

"Let's just leave the matter, Brian."

"What's the big deal anyway?" asked Elizabeth.

"There isn't any big deal, dear. Martha wanted to go to the club with your father and me for dinner

and I thought it would be a good idea if we all went
— you and Duncan too."

"I don't like the club."

"What do you like?"

"I like Cass." It didn't seem like the time to bring
the whole thing up again, but for the life of her,
Elizabeth couldn't stop herself from saying those
words.

"It isn't going to work." Mr. Douglass walked out
of the room.

Elizabeth watched her mother's eyes carefully.
Something really was up.

"Dad wasn't talking about Cass just then, was
he?"

"No." With a sigh Mrs. Douglass looked at Elizabeth sprawled on the sofa. "We've talked to Duncan
about taking you to your graduation. We thought
that since — "

"Duncan! He's my cousin, Mom! Duncan? To my
graduation?"

"We thought you two got along so well each
summer that — "

"He's my cousin and he's — he's — well, he's just
Duncan! It's a big N-O, no! God, Mother, where do
you get your bright ideas?" But she didn't wait for
an answer. She got up from the sofa and left the
room.

The door chimes rang twice — Aunt Martha's signal before she opened the door and walked in.
Elizabeth could hear them laughing in the hallway
and she thought she heard Duncan mumble some-

thing. Then she couldn't hear any voices. Her mother must be giving them the word about the afternoon's argument, she thought.

From the top of the stairs she could see Duncan's blond head, which almost brushed against the chandelier. When his father was alive he'd tried to inspire Duncan to be a basketball player, but with no success. He had the height, all right, but his co-ordination was more like a drunken giraffe's.

"There she is," her mother announced.

"Hiya," said Duncan.

"Howdy," returned Elizabeth, but no one seemed to notice the joke in that. She could hardly believe that anyone actually said "hiya" anymore. Somehow, at the beach Duncan didn't seem as awkward.

"I guess everybody here knows that the answer is no. Thanks for the thought, Duncan, but Mom forgot this one detail: I want to go with Cass and if Mom and Dad say I can't, then I won't go at all. No offense."

"That's a little drastic, isn't it, Elizabeth?" Aunt Martha was reapplying lipstick at the hallway mirror.

"That's the way it is."

"Let's all just go to the club and have a nice dinner and we can talk about this later." Mrs. Douglass said.

"Could I stay home?" Elizabeth watched the dust settle after she dropped that bomb.

"What's the sense of having her with us if she's going to keep up this foolishness?" Mr. Douglass said. "Aren't we all a little tired of this anyway?"

"I'll stay to keep you company," said Duncan. He gave a sideways look at his mother and then half smiled at Elizabeth. There was a hint of something strange in that smile, but maybe it only meant he would be just as bored as she would be at the club.

Elizabeth knew she would be pushing things too far if she said she didn't want Duncan to stay. "Sure, okay," was all she could manage politely.

When the car pulled out of the driveway Elizabeth finally turned from the front door and faced Duncan. He grinned a weird grin that, if she didn't know him better, she might have taken as a kind of conspiratorial signal.

"You hungry?"

"Not much," he said. "Got anything to drink?"

Elizabeth went to the kitchen and poked her head into the fridge. "Ginger ale. Orange juice. Milk."

"I mean a drink drink."

"What do you mean?" Then the idea began to sink in. "As in *booze?*" She couldn't believe her ears. Duncan asking for booze!

He smirked and headed into the dining room, aiming straight for her parents' bar. After a few moments of rattling he drew out a large bottle filled with something clear. "Vodka." He smirked again. "Get that orange juice."

"Wait a minute, Duncan. That'll never work. They'll know." She was starting to panic. How long would dinner at the club last anyway? Duncan had flipped!

"Just get the orange juice," he repeated, holding

out two of her mother's favourite glasses.

Still Elizabeth hadn't moved.

"Follow me." Rounding the corner toward the kitchen, Duncan knocked against the threshold and the two glasses gave a small ting.

Quickly Elizabeth rushed after him. "Let me carry those. Duncan, we — I mean, you — "

But already he had rummaged for the orange juice and had lined up the two glasses and the very large bottle on the counter. Into the glasses went a stream of vodka, which he then drowned with orange juice, finally plopping two ice cubes on top. Proudly he presented Elizabeth with a drink and then gave a toast: "To the Boston Red Sox."

Elizabeth watched him gulp his drink. She shuddered. This must be a dream, a bad dream.

"Come on. Try it. It tastes just like orange juice."

She did. He was right.

"But what about the bottle? They'll know."

Slyly Duncan poured vodka into a measuring cup. Into another he poured tap water. Like a magician he held the two cups together, then poured the water into the vodka bottle. "Voilà!"

They had another drink.

Elizabeth had a fuzzy feeling just underneath the roots of her hair. Her mind was thinking thoughts by itself but all she could say was, "I don't know. I just don't know."

The stereo was blaring.

Duncan, with another new drink in his hand, was slouched in a corner of the sofa.

"Do you do this all the time?" she asked.

"Mmm." He stared dumbly at his drink.

"Doesn't your mother find out?"

"Who cares?" He drew in his long legs and leaned against his knees. "Mom gets to me."

"You're different."

"Huh?"

"I mean, like this. Drinking. You're different."

"So're you," replied Duncan in a mumble.

"As soon as your mother was gone. Bam! You sure changed."

Duncan chuckled and gulped some more vodka and orange juice. "Let's dance." He gathered his lanky body up to almost a steady height and held out his hand to Elizabeth.

"Dance? You mean now? But it — " This was getting more ridiculous every minute, Elizabeth knew. "Nah. I can't dance right now."

"Okay," said Duncan and he started dancing with his glass pressed against his cheek.

When the song ended he held the empty glass up to the light and scrutinized it. "Time for a refill." He stumbled out to the kitchen.

The clock on the mantle chimed ten times. It couldn't be! thought Elizabeth with renewed panic. She rushed out to check the clock on the kitchen stove — it was never wrong. Ten o'clock. And Duncan was pouring another drink! She'd had two but she'd lost count of how many he had downed. A stupid grin was smeared across his face as he turned with his glass filled to the brim.

He's drunk! That fact had a very sobering effect

on Elizabeth and she searched her brain for what to do.

"Woody!" she said out loud and dialled his number, hoping he'd forgotten the argument of the night before. This was a thousand times worse!

Duncan tottered on the edge of the kitchen stool next to the breakfast counter. He watched her with a dumb curiosity.

"Hi. Thank God you answered the phone. I'm in trouble. Can you get over here quick? . . . No, it isn't Cass. Please, Woody, just come over . . . Okay, good." She hung up and looked at Duncan, who was staring down into his drink.

A few minutes later the kitchen door opened. Elizabeth nodded toward Duncan. "This is my cousin Duncan. This is Woody."

"Hiya," grinned Duncan.

"Oh-oh," said Woody.

"He's got this trick he does with water and vodka," explained Elizabeth. "Mom and Dad and Aunt Martha went out for dinner and we stayed here and — well, you can see the rest."

"When are they coming home?"

"Dinner was supposed to be at eight."

"Oh-oh."

"What about a shower?" suggested Elizabeth.

"That only works in the movies. The guy's drunk. He'll stay that way for quite a few hours."

"Oh, no," moaned Elizabeth.

"Hold it. Hold it," said Duncan grandly, manoeuvring himself off the stool. "I can handle this. No problem." He lurched, and just in time Woody grasped the glass. "Steady, steady," Duncan instructed himself, then laughed.

"You know what I said about being honest with your parents and trying to talk about things? Well, this might be the time to start," Woody said to Elizabeth.

"You can't be serious. They wouldn't understand."

"What else can you do?"

"Get rid of Duncan. You take him to your place. I'll say you came over here and you guys went somewhere. When he sobers up, send him home in a cab."

"No problem," muttered Duncan.

"How much did he drink anyway?"

"This measuring cup was full."

"And he's still standing?"

"Not quite," said Elizabeth, noting that at the moment it was the stove that was keeping Duncan upright. "What'll we do?"

But there was no time for an answer. The front door opened suddenly and in the hall they heard the cheerful voices of Elizabeth's mother, her father and her aunt.

Woody started to say something, then realized he had nothing to say. Blood drained from Elizabeth's face. Duncan took a last swallow of vodka and orange juice and dropped the glass. There was a melodic ting as it smashed.

"What was that? Elizabeth, are you — " Mrs. Douglass stopped mid-sentence. Behind her, Aunt Martha and Mr. Douglass peered into the kitchen, taking in the situation in seconds.

"Duncan?" His mother's voice was more a question than an exclamation.

Mrs. Douglass stared at the pieces of glass on the floor at Duncan's feet.

"There's an explanation," said Elizabeth, casting a quick glance at Woody. He nodded in encouragement.

"And there's no need for us to hear it," replied Mr. Douglass in exasperation. "Elizabeth, I want you to go to your room. Martha, please take your son home. And I won't even ask what you're doing here, Woody."

"Maybe you should listen to it anyway, sir," said Woody cautiously. "Elizabeth called because Duncan — " He stopped as Duncan's elbow began to slide across the stove.

"It's obvious what Duncan's problem is. And it's obvious where they got the alcohol too. I wasn't born yesterday, you know!"

"Let's take time to hear what they have to say, Brian," pleaded Mrs. Douglass. She was hoping things might not sound as bad as they looked.

"I certainly want an explanation," said Aunt Martha indignantly.

"Okay, okay." Mr. Douglass folded his arms across his chest and nodded at Elizabeth.

"Well, you guys left and then Duncan — that is, he — we — " She couldn't find the words to make this any easier on Duncan. "He happened to find the vodka and we thought we'd try a little bit of it with orange juice. We just — "

Somehow she knew this version of the truth wasn't working.

Then Duncan gave a small moan, took a few shaky steps toward the back door and threw up.

Elizabeth lay in her bed and stared into the blackness of her room. Although it was the middle of the night, she couldn't sleep. What a mess! In more ways than one!

After Aunt Martha had escorted Duncan to the bathroom and then to her car, Mr. Douglass had held the door open for Woody to make a silent exit. Then he had turned to Elizabeth and said, "You betrayed our trust tonight. Your mother and I are very disappointed — and hurt."

All the common sense she could muster told her to try to tell the complete unedited truth. But her tongue was tied in a double reef knot. Nothing, even in the deepest part of her soul, convinced Elizabeth that her parents would understand. They'd probably even find a reason to blame Duncan's binge on Cass!

"Do you have anything to say for yourself?"

She could hear the musical sound the pieces of glass made as her mother threw them into the garbage. Under the circumstances, all Elizabeth could think to reply to her father was, "Nothing. I've got nothing to say. It's too complicated."

"About as complicated as a one-way street," scoffed Mr. Douglass. "Go to your room. Maybe some time by yourself will give you a chance to think."

And he'd been right. She did think. She thought about Duncan throwing up. Gross!

She thought about Woody too. He was wrong about one thing, she knew. Talking to her parents honestly wouldn't help things at all. They only saw what they wanted to see.

And she thought about Cass. Going to the graduation dance with him seemed about as likely as going with him for a walk across the grey, bleak face of the moon.

Just before she fell asleep Elizabeth had an image of Woody storming away from her the night before. Boy, was he mad! And in her last drowsy seconds she saw him standing in her kitchen appraising the Duncan problem just minutes after she'd phoned for help. Thank goodness Woody didn't stay mad for long!

May 26

"Graduation tickets go on sale soon." As soon as Woody spoke the words he wondered why. It really had nothing to do with his mother.

Her noncommittal response verified this. "Mmm," she muttered as she opened the fridge.

Then he said, "Don't know whether I'll go."

"Why not?" She kicked the fridge door shut and balanced a lettuce, two tomatoes, some radishes and a large cucumber in her arms.

"Who'll I take?" Finally it was out.

His mother placed the salad ingredients in front of him. "Do you have to have a date? Oh, of course you do. You wouldn't want to go alone. That's stupid of me." She placed the cutting board and knife next to the vegetables. Then she left the kitchen.

Woody started peeling the cucumber, slicing thin, long, vertical strips, thinking about what it would be like to go to the dance alone. Picking himself up would be a cinch. No eagle-eyed father to give him the once-over as he stood on the front doorstep. He'd be on time too. And he wouldn't worry about whether he'd be too short. But when it came to asking himself to dance, he'd have to say no.

His mother breezed back into the kitchen. "Leave some cucumber rind on that, Woody, for colour." Then she added, "Why not just find a friend who also doesn't have a date?"

"Sounds boring," muttered Woody.

"Be more boring to stay home alone."

But her words "find a friend" made him think of Elizabeth. It looked pretty definite that she wasn't going to get to go with Cass — or with Duncan, for that matter. It wouldn't be like a real date.

Then, for some strange reason, he was thinking of when he used to have the wildest, most passionate crush on Elizabeth. Actually it had lasted right up to about grade six — from the time he'd loaned her his double-holster laser shooter with the anti-gravity ring to when Thelma Risser had moved into the neighbourhood for three short months. Just long enough for him to realize there were more girls in the world than the one who'd been his neighbour all his life.

He thought about the time she'd caught him using his magnifying glass to burn his initials with hers onto an old piece of board. He'd been concentrating so hard on getting the curve of the *D* just right that he hadn't heard Elizabeth coming up the street — and she'd been on rollerblades. She was about three seconds by wheel away from him when he knew he'd been caught in the act. Of course there was nothing else to do but run like an escaped convict and disappear into his basement. From the dusty window, by standing on his father's workbench, he had watched her pick up the piece of board, read it, skate away with it, only to finally toss it into the grass in front of the Jacobsons', who never mowed their lawn. A guy couldn't stay in a basement forever, Woody had known, but he could give it a good try.

And when he'd seen her the next day he'd braced himself for whatever he deserved, but she never mentioned it. Not ever. As a matter of fact, she managed not to say one word to him about anything for weeks.

The knife blade split the velvet red of the tomato and a smooth slice flopped onto the cutting board. Then another, and another.

If he did ask Elizabeth she'd say no. Not because of that dumb *WH loves EMD* burned into the wood when they were in grade four, but because of Cass. She really meant it when she said she was going with Cass or she wasn't going at all.

"I could ask Elizabeth." He surprised himself by saying it out loud. "Her folks won't let her go with Cass."

"Now there's a lovely idea, Woody. Why don't you do just that?"

"But people would think it was like a real date if I asked her."

"What does that matter? If you have no one you can think of to take to the prom, and if Elizabeth is not permitted to go with that boy — "

"Cass."

"Cass. Well, then I can't see why you two couldn't go together. I think it's perfectly fine for friends to go to a prom together."

"You're old-fashioned, Mom," said Woody, chopping a radish.

"Old-fashioned or not, I'd say missing your one and only prom was not worth — "

"Okay, okay. I get your point. Maybe I'll ask her."

"Good." Mrs. Harris opened the oven and removed an apple pie that was brown and bubbly.

But when Woody put the tossed salad into the fridge, doubts came back. It was loser material to ask just a friend to your graduation. Even Elizabeth would think that.

With a startling *brring* the telephone rang and his mother answered it. "It's for you."

As he picked up the phone his mother made a face at him and mouthed some command.

"Hello."

"Hi. It's Elizabeth."

Mrs. Harris was still pointing madly and making gestures that could only mean he should ask Elizabeth now. And he had a strange urge to do just that.

"Hey, I was thinking of calling you."

"What about? Duncan? Are you mad at me about Duncan too, Woody? I — I tried to tell Dad all about it, but — well, you saw what he was like. He doesn't want to hear anything. I know what you mean about talking to him and Mom, really I do. But it just won't work."

Woody gave his mother a cool stare. She caught the hint and discreetly left the room.

"Are you still there?" asked Elizabeth.

"Yeah, I'm here." He lowered his voice. "Mom was just here for a minute, that's all. So what happened with Duncan? Boy, I'd hate to have his head today."

"He's grounded until he can collect his old age pension. Aunt Martha just about freaked. She kept saying, 'If your father were alive' — like that was going to make Duncan collapse with guilt. All he could do was groan. Do people's eyes get crossed when they're that drunk?"

"How should I know?"

"His sure were crossed." Then she began to laugh. "Now that it's the next day it seems funny."

Woody said nothing.

"You're not mad at me, are you?"

"The fact that you've got an alcoholic cousin doesn't seem like the kind of thing to get mad at you about."

"But I called you and then Mom and Dad came home and — "

"Forget it."

"Thanks, Woody." Then she suddenly remembered what he'd said. "Hey, you said you were thinking of calling me. What for?"

"Oh, yeah." Woody was positive the idea of asking her to the dance was not going to go over well. But all the same, neither of them had a date.

Maybe this was the only solution. Desperation would soon be setting in. "Er — I was — ah — thinking about our grad dance. Since you don't have a date and neither do I — well, I got to thinking that maybe I would ask you to go with me."

Elizabeth said nothing.

"It was sort of Mom's idea," he added weakly, "but I didn't see anything wrong with it really."

"I'm going with Cass."

"I thought — I mean — "

"Somehow," Elizabeth insisted, "I'm going with him."

A dreamlike image appeared to Woody of that old piece of board with those scorched initials arching up into the air and disappearing into the mangled grass in front of the Jacobsons'. Elizabeth was rollerblading off down the sidewalk as he peered out through the basement window.

He cleared his throat and said in an overly confident way, "Now that I've asked you, I see it was a dumb idea. Just forget the whole thing, okay?"

"Yeah. Well, I am going to go with Cass." Her voice was awkwardly hesitant and Woody knew that she wouldn't forget this at all. "So — well, I gotta go do my math."

"Sure. See you tomorrow then."

"Bye.

Before he placed the receiver back on the hook Woody realized he'd reopened something he wished he hadn't. He hoped it wouldn't be the disaster he'd begun with his magnifying glass way back in grade four.

"Let's think of someone else to ask," said his mother, sauntering back into the kitchen, trying to be nonchalant.

"Let's not think, Mom." He escaped upstairs to his headphones.

May 30

Exams.

That word struck fear in every heart. Except for the teachers, of course. They dropped it like tiny nuclear bombs whenever they could. *This will be on the exam . . . If you don't know this for the exam . . . This is the last time we'll review this before the exam.*

Exams were two weeks away. All the excitement of graduation had to be pushed aside till exams were over.

At lunchtime the graduation committee was frantically making decorations that would miraculously transform the gymnasium into a carnival, complete with cotton candy and a carousel. That was the theme this year. Gigantic half-painted paper merry-go-round horses sprawled on the floor with two or three people leaning over them filling in browns, reds, startling blues and purples, and a grimace of white teeth.

Elizabeth was sitting cross-legged, pulling at

tufts of cotton balls to make them fluffy, and Carolyn was mixing pink paint the colour of cotton candy. Woody was making cone-shaped handles and trying to ignore the fact that Elizabeth wasn't talking to him. She hadn't even looked in his direction once.

"Speaking of exams," Woody said to no one in particular, "did anyone see the extra-help questions Johnston gave on *King Lear?*"

"King who?" replied Carolyn with an exaggerated squint of her eyes.

"They were tough. Shakespeare couldn't answer them."

"Shakespeare takes Miss Johnston out to dinner on Saturdays," said Carolyn, "and gives her the inside story on what he meant."

"This cotton candy idea isn't going to work." Elizabeth let a piece of cotton ball drift to the floor.

"It'll be up on the wall," said Woody, looking through the hole at the bottom of the first cone he'd made successfully.

"And it'll be dark too," Carolyn added. She dotted the cotton ball with a blotch of pink, then leaned back critically.

"Hey, Elizabeth, come here!" shouted someone from the other side of the art room. "Is the Ferris wheel supposed to be this big?"

With a sigh she got up to investigate.

"Did she tell you about Sunday night?" asked Woody.

"Mmm," murmured Carolyn, arranging some cotton candy on top of a cone.

"Well?"

"Well what?"

"Do you know what I'm talking about?"

"You asked her to go to the grad with you." Still she concentrated on the cotton candy.

"And now she acts like I'm Frankenstein."

"Dr. Jeckle and Mr. Hyde."

"Huh?"

"She thinks there's the you that we see every day and another you that's somehow different."

"I knew it. I just knew it. She thinks I've got a thing for her, doesn't she? That's just great. Mom and her big ideas. I'm going to set her straight."

"Here she comes. And here I go." Carolyn picked up some cotton and paint and scrambled away.

"Elizabeth — " he began, standing up.

"Look, Woody — "

"No, you look. Carolyn sort of told me you think I've got this thing for you. I don't. It was Mom's idea that I ask a friend and I thought it was a good one. It wasn't. And I'm sick of how you've been going around all week like I'm some kind of weirdo. Well, I hope you get to the grad with Cass or Duncan or whoever takes you, but I'm sorry I asked."

He dropped the cardboard cone on the floor beside the others and left the room, not giving her a chance to say anything.

Elizabeth left the dinner table and went directly to her room. It was one of the benefits of pre-exam nights that her parents didn't expect her to help with the dishes. She tried to study but couldn't concentrate. At last she gave up and called Cass.

"Hi. It's me."

"Hi. What's new?"

"Not much." She had still not told him the gory details about Duncan and Saturday night, nor about Woody asking her to the graduation dance. Why complicate things? "We finished the carousel today. Wait'll you see it."

Cass sighed. "Look, Elizabeth. About the dance. It's pretty late to be thinking I'll be allowed to take you. I want to — but your parents — "

"I don't need to go to the stupid dance," she interrupted.

"It's your graduation. You have to go."

"You didn't go to yours."

"But I didn't pass either. There's no sense in going to graduation if you don't pass."

"It's just a dance. Who cares?"

Cass sighed again and she could tell he was about to say something, but he stopped just in time.

"How's my helmet?" she asked, to break the silence.

"Still lookin' good."

"Hey, Cass," she said, "I've just thought of something!"

"What?"

"Tonight Mom and Dad are going to a movie. They go every Thursday. They'll be leaving in about half an hour, so why don't I meet you somewhere?"

"Hold on, Elizabeth. I don't know. You're supposed to be studying and — "

"I know all this stuff. All I'm doing is staring at the books anyway. An hour or two won't make any difference."

"But what about your parents?"

"How'll they know? If I get back by ten that's a good two hours before they come home. Come on, Cass. Don't be so lame."

"Okay, okay. But I've got a feeling this'll get us in even more trouble."

"What could possibly happen? Meet me over at Frankie's. And bring my helmet. I want another ride."

Cass was sitting on his bike waiting for her when she got to Frankie's. It was good to give him a big hug and feel the cool leather of his jacket against her face.

"Wanna go inside?" she asked. "I haven't beat you in the frog game for quite a while."

"Aw, not the frog game. Aren't you sick of that old has-been yet?"

"You're just saying that because I always win. And it's not a has-been. It's a classic. There's a difference — like with your bike."

"Don't go saying my bike's anything like that game."

Elizabeth laughed and took Cass's hand.

Hardly anyone she knew from school was there, even though it was early. Exams. They swallowed up students and kept them hostage for some of the best nights of the year — especially spring nights.

"Hi, Frankie," they said in unison.

Standing beside the frog game, Elizabeth said, "You go first."

"We'll flip for it," returned Cass, seeing through her strategy. "Heads you get to watch the warm-up game. Tails I do." He spun a coin into the air.

"Heads . . . like I said, you go first." She grinned.

The animated highway on the video screen was busy with cars and trucks of all colours and shapes streaming past. A green frog squatted at the side of the road ready for Cass to manoeuvre it across the traffic to the safety of the row of shelters at the other side. It hopped successfully to the meridian. A car passed a truck, narrowly missing Cass's frog as it leapt onto the grey of the highway. Two quick hops to the passing lane, a sideways one, then three springing leaps to the shelter.

Instantly a second frog appeared on the side of the highway. One, two, three stretched leaps and an abrupt stop as a fat-wheeled jeep sped past. One leap more, then from out of nowhere appeared a blue car. *Splat!* The green frog disappeared.

At the end of the game Cass had safely guided six of the eight frogs into the shelters. 61,339 points.

"Your turn."

Elizabeth stood in front of the game confidently. The first frog made the meridian in two leaps without a brush with death. From there it leapt, paused to avoid a truck, leapt, leapt, leapt and grinned from the shelter.

"Not bad. But that's only one," said Cass.

The next glowing green frog ventured onto the

highway. *Sprong*. It was caught in mid-leap by the blur of a speeding red sports car. Cass laughed at Elizabeth's muttered exclamation.

The third frog hopped onto the highway and bounced sideways twice to get into position to make a leap for the safety of mid-boulevard. A car! Hop, hop, hop, with a frantic series of quick movements of Elizabeth's right hand, and the frog was safe.

"Phew," she said, concentrating.

"It's only a frog," teased Cass.

"A girl can never be sure when one'll turn out to be a prince." She leaned into the game with full attention on the steady stream of vehicles that threatened to lose the game for her.

At last frog number eight squatted, waiting. Cass had lost two frogs. So far, she'd lost only one. She gulped a lungful of air and directed the frog out into the traffic, just behind a tractor-trailer. A hop, a leap and a quick lunge before two cars, one passing the other, came suddenly onto the screen. The frog gained the safety of the grassy meridian. *Sprong*. Another car went past without incident. Hop, hop, hop. The road was free ahead. Leap. Almost there. Hop — *splat!*

"That one'll never know if he was a prince," laughed Cass.

Elizabeth concentrated on the points. 63,282! "I beat you!"

"Lucky. Let's go."

"No challenge?" she asked as he took her hand warmly.

"You've got an in with frogs," he said. "Especially old has-been ones."

Elizabeth raised her elbow to poke him playfully in the ribs and he swerved out of reach, laughing.

When they got outside she placed her new purple helmet over her long hair, brushing it back before doing up the chin strap.

"Where to? It's only twenty-five after nine," said Cass.

"Just around."

"Let's go for a burger."

"Okay." Elizabeth stretched her arms around Cass and held the leather of his jacket in her fists.

Even riding through city streets, being on the back of Cass's bike was a thrill. When he revved the 750 Elizabeth lurched in resistance to the sudden speed. She clung even more tightly, laughing. In a dramatic lean they turned into the takeout.

"Let's eat out here at these tables," she said, pulling off her helmet and running her thin fingers through her tangled hair.

A few small birds, used to handouts, hopped around near their table and Cass threw bits of hamburger bun to one mangy sparrow. Elizabeth could tell there was something on his mind.

Finally he leaned over the table, squeezing the empty milkshake carton between his palms, and said, "You know, Elizabeth, university is a lot of fun. Look at my brother. He says there are parties every night and everybody goes. He even hates coming home for Christmas."

"I won't be like that. I'll come home as often as I

can. It's not that far." She studied his eyes, trying to read the thoughts behind his words.

"You might change your mind when you get there."

"Is that what you think? That as soon as I get to university I'll forget about us?"

"Well, not exactly. At least you won't on purpose."

"I won't at all."

He stared at the squashed milkshake container. Then he turned to her and smiled. Reaching one arm around her neck he pulled her head toward him in a kind of wrestling grip and roughed her hair lightly with his other hand. "You got the whole thing figured out, haven't you, Brains?"

"Yeah," she said confidently and untangled herself from his grip. She kissed his mouth lightly. And then she kissed him again.

"Well, it's gonna take the best work your brain can manage to get your folks to change their minds about me — and about the grad. I bet they hope you'll get to university and meet some guy and forget about me."

"Who cares what they hope?"

June 3

Woody couldn't budge. His was the lower locker and three people hemmed him in — one on each side and one reaching over him, almost knocking off his glasses. It was like this every day at the end of school, especially Mondays when the homework was usually piled on heavy.

Suddenly he felt a poke in his side, but when he turned around to see who had poked him he got an elbow in the face. As soon as he went back to rummaging through his locker it happened again. "Hey!" He whirled around, just about giving himself a case of whiplash.

Through the wall of bodies he saw a slim, pale, beautiful girl with long straight black hair. She was smiling at him. He didn't know her name but he'd noticed her before. Who wouldn't?

"Hi, Woody," she said. Her voice was even and cool.

"Hi."

"I want to ask you something," she said as he

finally made his way out of the tangle of bodies at the lockers.

"First I want to ask *you* something," he said in a voice that surprised him with its confidence. "What's your name?"

"Sonia Bethany Morrison." She smiled as if she had a secret.

Woody was falling in love. He smiled back.

"Now can I ask you what I wanted to ask you?"

"Sure."

"You may already have invited someone but — well, in case you haven't I'll ask anyway. Would you take me to graduation? I mean, I'm only in grade ten and I'm not graduating but I really would like to go and I thought if you — "

"You want *me* to take you to graduation?" Woody lost control of his lower jaw and his mouth gaped open. "The answer is a positive yes," he said as soon as he recovered from the shock. "But it seems strange that — I mean, there must be other guys you'd want to ask. You don't even know me, so why do you want me to take you? I'm still saying yes. It's just that — "

She laughed, wrinkling her eyes and swinging her shiny-as-licorice hair back over her shoulders. Her teeth were an even row of white pearls.

Woody was sinking further and further into love every second.

"We have time to get to know each other a bit before the dance," she said with a sly smile. "It doesn't have to be a blind date."

"Yeah. Well, you're right." He stared at her.

"Maybe you could help me with my history. You could come to my place."

Woody forgot to answer. His mind had already taken him to Sonia's house, wherever it was, and placed him beside her at a dimly lit table where, his hand placed warmly over hers, their heads leaning suggestively close, he instructed her on the strategies of the Roman invasion of Britain in 55 B.C. Sonia's deep brown eyes gazed at him thankfully.

"My mother would like to meet the boy who takes me to the dance before graduation night anyway. She's buying me a new dress."

"And I'd like to meet her if she's as beautiful as her daughter," said Woody, quoting from some repeat movie he'd seen on late-night TV, not feeling in the least embarrassed to be saying a line like that. This really must be what it's like to be in love, he decided.

"Can I carry your books home?" he offered. How could such long eyelashes be suspended over such perfect, intense eyes?

She gave him that laugh again. "No, my friends are waiting. They didn't think I'd have the nerve to ask you."

Her glance behind Woody directed his attention to three girls who were standing down the hall trying not to look obvious when actually they were glued to what was happening in front of Woody's locker. He waved. One waved back and the two others laughed. He figured once he got to know Sonia better he'd naturally get to know her friends too. Might as well start off being friendly.

"Well, give me your phone number. I might like to call you up. Not tonight, but maybe soon," he said with a casual air. It was clear she already liked him, so he could take a chance on playing a bit nonchalant about calling her.

"Here," she said, handing him a page from her notebook with her phone number neatly written beside her name.

"Okay. Well, I guess I'll be talking to you. Take it easy on the old history book," he joked weakly.

She laughed and joined her friends. As soon as the four girls were out of sight Woody turned back to his locker, but he forgot what he'd been looking for. Maybe it was science. No, there was no science homework. Math? All he could think about was whether he remembered enough about Roman roads to teach Sonia if she asked him. And there wasn't even anyone around he really knew to tell this whole thing to.

He slammed his locker shut and hurried off to find anyone who might be walking home in his direction and who had two good ears.

June 4

The morning was a drizzly, dreary one but Elizabeth got up early with a plan to intercept Woody on his way to school. She hoped he'd forgotten all about the grad invitation by now and things could get back to normal.

As she walked near his driveway she heard garbage cans clanging and then a familiar voice moaning a desperate, "Awwww." In a minute she was at the source of the sound. Woody was just struggling to his feet amidst the rubbish from an overturned garbage can and compost bin, his sneakers buried somewhere in the mess.

"You all right?" she asked.

He shook a banana peel from the toe of his sneaker. "Why do kids, not parents, have to put out garbage? Is there a home on this entire continent where garbage is taken out by parents?" he said, not actually to Elizabeth, more to the unsympathetic universe at large.

Mrs. Harris appeared at the side door. "Woody?

Was that you making all that racket?"

"Yes and no," he replied with a certain amount of control. "But I wouldn't ask for details if I were you, Mom."

"Oh. Hi, Elizabeth. How are you, dear? All prepared for the exams, I suppose?" She peered around the open door. Mrs. Harris was always smiling.

"Yes — well, I'm not too worried, I guess," Elizabeth replied.

"Do get that mess cleaned up, Woody," said his mother. Then she turned to Elizabeth. "That's a lovely rain jacket. I can't get Woody to wear one. Do you remember when you got that bright blue raincoat and matching boots, Elizabeth? Let's see, you both must've been in grade two. You came knocking on the door just after supper. Your mother had phoned to tell me you had it in your mind to try out the new rain suit, so I got Woody all bundled up and gave him my umbrella. Off you went, the two of you, like little lost children in the rain. Once around the block and you were back for hot cocoa and lemon pie. Seems like only yesterday."

"Yesterday, Mom, I asked you to make me a lemon pie and you told me I'd get fat," said Woody.

"You did no such thing. Don't you believe him, Elizabeth. That boy teases so!" She closed the door with a grin.

"Here, I'll help you," offered Elizabeth, picking up two tins.

When all the garbage was sorted again, Woody

lifted the garbage can with a grunt and started to walk to the curb. Elizabeth followed. "You wanna wheel that compost bin down for me?" he asked.

Watching him shuffling along in front of her she was glad she'd decided not to mention anything about his invitation to the dance. She'd thought about it when she first woke up that morning. She'd had half a plan to say something to him that would smooth things over, in case he was still mad. It didn't seem like he was bugged anymore.

Woody looked with disgust at something unidentifiable and gooey on his hands. "Give me a minute to wash. I presume you happened by to go to school with me. As long as we don't mention movies, Cass, your parents or political patronage I'll agree to walk with you. Besides, I've got a bit of hot news. You're off the hook about the grad — old Romeo Harris has a real date."

"What?"

He grinned and disappeared into the house.

"So who is she?" Elizabeth barely gave him time to get back outside.

"Sonia Morrison. Miss Sonia Bethany Morrison," he said.

"Who's she?"

"A beautiful — no, scratch that — a charismatic beauty. She happens to be in grade ten and finally swallowed all her girlish shyness and stopped me in the hall and asked me to take her to the grad. Ah, the wise little lady."

"She asked you?"

"Certainly. Are you surprised?"

"Well, yes. I mean . . . When we get to school show me who she is. I want to get a look at her."

"There she is," he said as soon as they walked through the doors. "Over there by the water fountain. With that bunch of girls."

"Which one is she?"

"See that cascade of velvet black hair?" he exaggerated.

"Oh, that one. I've seen her around. Usually near the boys' locker room."

"What's that supposed to mean?"

"Come on, let's go over and talk to her."

"What? Now? What for?"

"Just to say hi, that's all."

Elizabeth edged Woody over to Sonia and her little crowd. Everyone smiled politely.

"Hi. Ah — Sonia, I'd like you to meet Elizabeth. She lives on my street."

"Hi," said Elizabeth.

"Hi. You go out with Tony Cassidy, don't you? I've seen you and him around," Sonia said sweetly.

"Yeah. I'm going with him," replied Elizabeth. She was surprised that she felt the need to claim Cass. Something in Sonia's eyes . . .

"He's really cute."

"Thanks." Really she wanted to say, "Lay off!"

When he and Elizabeth were far enough away from Sonia and her group, Woody asked, "Did I catch a bit of feminine intuition stirring your mind just then?"

"No comment."

"Not fair."

"I'm not sure what I'm thinking anyway. Maybe it's all wrong."

"Give me a hint."

"Love is blind."

"That's a hint?"

"Yeah. Now, don't ask me any more."

"You don't like Sonia?"

"I hardly know her."

"But you don't like her anyway. You don't think I should take her to the grad."

"Did I say that? You can take whoever you want. It's your business."

"Right. Let's keep it that way," he said bluntly.

An ear-blasting ring sounded through the halls — the last bell before morning announcements. The few stragglers began to run to their classes.

"Please just forget what I said, Woody," Elizabeth called as they parted. "I'm glad you've got a date. Really I am."

As morning announcements began she tried to put a nagging thought out of her head. But the persistent feeling that Sonia would mean trouble could not be buried.

June 6

When her parents left for the movies that Thursday Elizabeth was out the door in a flash on her way to meet Cass. He was in front of Frankie's, sitting on the Honda, waiting, polishing the side of Elizabeth's purple helmet with the sleeve of his grey sweatshirt.

"Hi, stranger," he said.

She gave him a light kiss in reply.

"Where to?"

"Let's go down to the field."

Elizabeth liked the rutted road that ran along the edge of the field and into the small clump of woods. It was used for biking, and for cross-country skiing in the winter. Here and there huge boulders poked out like giant fists, making the ride a thrill of twists and bumps. The road was no problem for Cass and his 750, though others often wiped out in a minute.

As always, Cass's bike took the old road with ease, dipping and leaning, groaning in low mutters as it slowed, and revving up to a smoother pitch when he increased the speed. After they had done the loop a few times Elizabeth shouted over Cass's shoulder, "Let me try!"

"What?" he yelled, stopping the bike.

"Let me drive."

"No way!"

"Come on, Cass. I already know how to drive it. You showed me."

"Yeah, but that was just showing. You never really drove. Not on a road like this. No way."

"Well, what if I just drive on the field?"

"Look, it's starting to get dark. I should take you back."

"Stop treating me like a little kid, Cass. Just across the field. That's not very far."

He couldn't think of a way to talk her out of it. There she was, grinning at him as if she knew everything. Under the purple helmet her smooth, pale complexion had a kind of glow. Maybe it was from the reflection of the setting sun. Around them the green grass had turned a rusty gold.

"Well?"

He looked across the field, trying to find a good reason to say no. Finally he gave in. "Okay. But go slow. Very slow. And I'll reach around to hold my hands over yours in case you turn the handle the wrong way."

"You'll break my neck doing that. Really, Cass, it's all right. I can do it. You get on back."

The bike sputtered underneath them. Cass put his arms around her waist and leaned over to give her last-minute instructions about where the gas and the brake were. "Go slow!" he yelled.

"I will!" shouted Elizabeth excitedly.

The bike jerked forward, then came to an abrupt stop.

"Sorry about that. I've just got to get the feel of this thing."

Again they eased forward, lurched, almost stopped, then smoothly built up a bit of momentum. The grassy field cushioned the ride.

"Now you've got it," said Cass. "Take up the speed a bit more. Not much!" he added with a shout when the bike bounded forward.

"Lean to the left!" yelled Elizabeth. "There's a hole up there."

"Just go round it! Easy!"

She leaned as they came near it, and turned the bike to the left. As she did, without meaning to she revved up on the gas. The bike gained speed instantly. Cass wasn't ready for it. Neither was Elizabeth.

"Slow down!" he warned.

"Lean with me!" she hollered.

"What are you doing?"

But it was too late. The bike was aimed at the hole and, although they weren't going very fast, there was no avoiding it. The front wheel skimmed the edge and the loose dirt gave way. The bike fell over, spilling Cass off and pinning Elizabeth under it.

Woody walked to Sonia's house feeling pretty much in control of life. The sleeves of his red sweater were tied casually, magazine-perfect, around his neck and the two buttons of his sports shirt were undone. His black cords were a little wrinkled, as if he'd worn them all day, though he hadn't. Since the night of Carolyn's party he hadn't smoked a cigarette. He'd been studying fairly regularly, so he was beginning to think he'd surprise a few people with some good marks, maybe even a couple of honours. At dinner that night his mother had agreed that it wasn't too extravagant to rent a tuxedo for the graduation dance. He could just see himself wearing it, a black satin cummerbund at his waist and a bright red bow tie so he wouldn't look like a waiter in a fancy restaurant. Sonia would be impressed.

The book under his arm reminded him that he was going to Sonia's house to help her get ready for her history exam. Brushing up on the Roman Empire he'd remembered that Julius Caesar had a few spicy things in his life that made his story worthwhile, like Cleopatra and Brutus. That was the way to teach Sonia — make history a story about lovers and friends.

Cass scrambled to his feet and switched off the motor. It sputtered and then was silent. Quickly he lifted the 750 off Elizabeth who, so far, had said nothing.

"You all right?" he asked frantically.

"I — my arm — oww." She lay back, her face a mask of pain. "Is — is the bike okay?"

"Sure. We weren't going that fast. Anyway, forget the bike! Here, let me take this off," he said, carefully unfastening her helmet. He helped her sit up.

She held her right arm close to her body. "Cass, I think it must be broken!" she said desperately, watching his face, knowing he was thinking, as she was, about what that would mean — explaining why she was out, why she was with Cass, why she was driving the bike.

"Is that the arm you write with?" he asked.

"Yes. There go exams!" She struggled not to cry, to keep the pain from getting to her.

"I think you're supposed to keep a broken arm still. Maybe we should strap it with this belt. Guess I'd better drive you down to emergency. Then we'll call your parents."

"No!" she shouted with new fear. "I don't want them to know!" Her fear was mixed with exasperation.

"Don't be crazy, Elizabeth. They'll have to know."

"But — " Tears began to well up in her eyes. "We can tell them I was at Carolyn's. That something happened there. I fell down the steps or something. Just take me to Carolyn's. Maybe her parents aren't home."

Cass tried to help her up without jarring her arm. "I don't know, Elizabeth. You need to see a doctor right away. If we go to Carolyn's — "

"We have to, Cass! We have to!" Now she was crying.

Elizabeth's tears always made Cass squirm and

try to find the easiest way to stop them. Unwillingly he agreed to try Carolyn's first. He picked up the bike and started it.

Carefully, her face held in a grimace of pain, Elizabeth managed to get on behind him.

In a night of crazy bad luck they got a break at Carolyn's — her parents weren't home. Just Carolyn and Belinda and they both swore to secrecy, hoping the doctor would believe Elizabeth had fallen down a few steps.

They cleaned the mud off her clothes and called a cab to take them to Emergency. Cass reluctantly stayed behind after Carolyn promised to call him as soon as the doctor had examined Elizabeth's arm.

"Hi, Woody," Sonia smiled at him as she opened the large oak door. Walking up the curved, stone pathway Woody had been impressed by the size of her home. It was big enough to house a baseball team and half their fans. The lawn looked as if someone planned to start a golf course.

"All set to find out about the life and times of Mr. J. Caesar?" he joked.

"All set. Come in." Sonia closed the door and walked in front of him, her perfume lingering, teasing his nostrils.

Before Woody was halfway down the hall Sonia's mother was there to greet him, her hand extended but her smile lukewarm. "I'm Sonia's mother, dear. She's told me all about you."

"Good evening, Mrs. Morrison," said Woody formally, taking hold of her thin, cool hand, feeling its many rings against his palm. He was thinking how little Sonia really knew about him. How much could she have said to her mother? He decided he'd just smile a lot and let Mrs. Morrison do the talking. "And you're graduating this year?"

Smile, small nod.

"My, my. You seem so young to be actually graduating."

Weak smile, no nod.

"And Sonia is very excited about the dance. We've bought her a darling dress."

Smile. This was getting easier by the minute, Woody thought.

All Sonia was doing was biting the end of her thumb.

"Well, I'd better let you two have some privacy so you can do history. That was always my worst subject, history. Like mother, like daughter, they say. But she gets very good marks in the long run." She brushed her hand along Sonia's silky black hair possessively.

Smile. He hoped Sonia wasn't much like her mother at all.

"Nice to meet you, dear."

"Nice to have met you too," he returned, thinking that total silence would have made him look like a moron. That was hardly the image to present when you were about to spend some quiet hours leaning close to a woman's daughter trying to teach her some history.

"We can study in the den," Sonia said smoothly,

leading the way into a room that looked like a corner of the public library. "This is really Daddy's room but he's away this week and I always use it while he's away."

She shut the door behind them.

"Nice," said Woody, gazing around at the volumes and volumes of hardcover books that were in rows of matched sets, some green with gold, some brown, some bright red. "Does your father read much?"

"As a matter of fact, yes. But a lot of these are just for show. Like these. They're all of Shakespeare's plays, and his poems too. Daddy bought them at an auction but he says he'll never read them."

"I don't like Shakespeare," Woody said.

"I like *Romeo and Juliet*. We studied that this year," said Sonia.

"I didn't like the set-up. She should've warned him she was taking that stuff to make her look dead. Poor communication."

"But that's what made the play a passionate love story." Her eyes twinkled at Woody.

"Speaking of story, let's do some history."

Sonia brought a second chair over to her father's desk and spread her scribbler notes and text in front of the two of them. Her knee touched Woody's and she smiled.

He smiled too, a weak quiver at the corner of his mouth. Then he cleared his throat and frowned as he leafed through her notes. "Where should we start?"

She leaned her face near Woody's, staring him in the eye, and said very directly, "Don't you want to know what it's like to kiss me?"

Woody was flabbergasted. But he quickly recovered and said, "Sure," though he still didn't move to kiss her. If she was joking he didn't want to fall for it.

"Well then, kiss me," she demanded, still looking at him as if they were discussing something ordinary like bread and jam.

This was no joke. He leaned toward her small mouth and tried to angle his glasses so they wouldn't smash into her nose. He kissed her. Her lips were warm and tasted like cinnamon. When he opened his eyes she was still staring at him. It made him think, absurdly, of a mirror. One of his best kept secrets was that when he was twelve or thirteen he had practised leaning toward a mirror and kissing his own reflection. He wanted to see what he looked like when he moved in for a kiss.

He sat back in the chair and looked at Sonia. She seemed intent on studying him. No nervous laugh, no cheeks pink with embarrassment. It wasn't easy to figure her out, he thought.

"Now shall we do some history?" he asked finally.

"Let's just kiss some more. I know all the history. I just used that as an excuse to invite you over when I should be studying for exams. Mother doesn't know that I really find history easy. It's like a story."

"Yeah. A story." Woody couldn't believe his ears.

Here was a beautiful girl telling lies so she could invite him to her house and kiss his lips numb. It was too good to be true.

"I like cinnamon better than history any day," he said.

The mahogany clock on the mantle was ticking, filling the room with its smooth sound. On the sofa sat Elizabeth, her right arm in a cast which reached from her wrist halfway to her shoulder. Mrs. Douglass was in the kitchen making coffee. Mr. Douglass was leaning against the mantle, gazing down into the empty fireplace as though there were a blazing, comforting fire there.

It was awkward. Getting into these situations was becoming a regular occurrence, thought Elizabeth.

"Here's some coffee. Elizabeth, do you want some? I'll put in cream and sugar for you."

Elizabeth didn't want to be the first one to talk about her broken arm. She felt that, somehow, they'd find out the truth. So she just sipped her coffee.

"Well, we've got a problem," said Mr. Douglass finally, turning from the fireplace to sit in the largest chair in the room. He looked like some kind of judge with his mouth set in a tight frown. His blue eyes seemed tired.

Elizabeth glanced at her mother, who was looking at the cast.

"Tell me, if you can," continued Mr. Douglass, "what it's going to take to get the message through to you."

Suddenly Elizabeth felt more angry and frustrated than scared. "You act like everything's so wrong! Like I'm totally irresponsible!"

"Take a look at that cast, Elizabeth. Have you forgotten that already? Or are you trying to say you were being responsible going out when we assumed you were safe at home studying. And then you shatter your arm in two places! Is that your idea of responsible? Because if it is, then I must be from another planet!" Getting up from his chair and brushing his hand impatiently through his hair, he found himself in front of the fireplace again with nothing to look at.

"Dear," said Mrs. Douglass calmly, yet with the strain of worry still in her voice, "let's not start a yelling match. Not tonight. It's just too much."

"Mom, I'm sorry. I really am. I know I didn't tell you where I was going. It was a stupid thing — " She couldn't help but think about how doubly stupid it would seem to both her parents if they knew the whole truth.

Mrs. Douglass stopped staring at the cast and sighed. "Maybe it wasn't so bad, dear." She gave Elizabeth a weak smile.

Elizabeth began to feel vaguely safe.

"And what exactly does that mean?" demanded Mr. Douglass.

"I'm not sure, Brian." She got up and walked over to her husband. "All she did was go to her friend's house. They did say they were studying together. We've allowed that before. If she hadn't fallen — "

"I can't believe my ears," Mr. Douglass said. "You're admitting you don't care that Elizabeth didn't tell us the truth. We've lost control of our own daughter." He extended his hands in a helpless gesture.

"We haven't lost control. But maybe it's time we gave her some control of her own. After all, she's growing up. She'll be graduating soon."

"So you're giving up."

"No, not giving up. Bending."

"Well, I'm not bending. Next thing I know you'll be allowing her to go out with that Tony character. I suppose that's the next thing!"

Elizabeth felt her heart sink at the mention of Cass. It was as though her secret would be found out any minute now.

Mr. Douglass placed his coffee cup noisily on the mantle. "As far as I'm concerned, until she has moved out of this house she will answer to her parents!" He started to leave the room.

"Turning your back on us isn't going to solve the problem, Brian."

He halted abruptly, a look of confused anger on his face. "You're too emotional because of Elizabeth's accident, Sandra. Tomorrow when things have calmed down you'll see that I'm right." He went into his study and closed the door.

Elizabeth watched her mother closely. She was gazing at the space where her husband had just been standing, as if she could still hear his words. In profile, her face was calm and beautiful. She seemed to have a new air of confidence.

Getting up from the sofa Elizabeth went to her mother. "Give me a hug, Mom. I love you." The large plaster-of-Paris cast was like a second person in her mother's arms.

Even in this secure closeness Elizabeth could only think about the bike, the accident and Cass. If she tried to tell the truth now her mother would be so hurt. And her father would really be right. It was too late now — the secret had to be kept.

"Why can't Dad understand, Mom?"

"Your father and I are afraid you'll make some unwise decisions."

"Like what?"

"Oh, like something that seems fine for now but that won't turn out to be so good for you later."

Elizabeth figured that meant Cass.

"At your age it's easy to do something that will affect the rest of your life — maybe in ways that aren't so good. Your father's not sure you realize that."

"I do! I can think things through for myself."

Mrs. Douglass reached out to touch a silky strand of her daughter's hair and twirled it gently in her fingers. "I hope so, Elizabeth. I hope so."

The wistful tone of her mother's voice made Elizabeth hesitate. How could she possibly know if what she decided now would be right for her later? How could anybody know that? And with her arm bound in the thick cast she could not forget the real reason it was broken. Maybe she wasn't so good at thinking about things for herself after all.

She lay her head against her mother and curled her good arm beneath the burden of the cast.

It was only ten o'clock but Woody felt as if it was two in the morning. His mouth was numb and his eyes were stinging for some reason, maybe from opening and closing them so many times. He was very hungry. Actually Sonia's mother had asked them half an hour ago if they'd like to have something to eat before Woody left but Sonia had quickly said no. They were too busy with Caesar and his Roman Empire. How could Woody disagree?

Now he was starving.

Just as he got to the takeout, drooling for a burger, extra cheese, no onions, Woody heard a bike behind him. It was Cass. But something was wrong. The bike was a mess, all muddy and with a dent in the gas tank. And Cass looked as though someone had started a nuclear war and he was the only one so far who knew about it.

"What happened to your bike?"

"We had a little accident, me and Elizabeth. Little for me — not so little for her. She broke her arm in two places."

"She okay?"

"Sort of. We were down at the field and she wanted to drive." He banged his fist against the handle bar. "Geez, what made me let her do that?"

"You were down at the field? But I thought you two weren't — "

"Her folks were out at a movie," interrupted

Cass. "She sneaked out last Thursday too."

Elizabeth was in a mess for sure, thought Woody. Worse than with Duncan. "How did her parents take it?"

"I'm not sure." Then he explained Elizabeth's plan to go to Carolyn's house and not tell her mother and father what really happened.

Woody decided not to say, "It figures." Why bother even thinking about how she handled her parents? She obviously wasn't planning to change. And through some rare stroke of luck he wasn't involved in this mess "Going in for a burger?" he asked.

"Nah. Just saw you and stopped. After Carolyn called me about what the doctor said I just wanted to get out of the house. Ride around a while. Think I'll head back home again and get the bike cleaned up."

"She'll be all right."

"Sure." Cass turned his bike away from the takeout and was soon out of sight.

Woody tried to switch his thoughts from Elizabeth's broken arm to a mouth-watering hamburger. But he wasn't hungry anymore. Knowing Elizabeth, she'd be right back at school the next day. He'd get all the details then. And, he promised himself, he wouldn't get on her case about lying. What was the use?

The house was quiet. Elizabeth was in bed. When Mrs. Douglass checked on her, her heart ached at the sight of the clumsy cast on her daughter's arm.

She made a pot of tea and arranged two cups and two muffins on a tray. What she had to say couldn't wait until tomorrow. Brian was still in his den, so she carried the tray in there. He looked up from where he was working at his desk, the green-shaded brass lamp the only light in the room.

"Let's have some tea."

He knew this meant she wanted to talk. It was an old habit of theirs. Sometimes arguments could be soothed by tea. They smiled weakly at each other. This was a way to begin.

"Is she asleep?" he asked, adding honey to his cup.

"I think so. Or pretending to be." She pulled a chair close to the desk.

"Lucky she wasn't knocked unconscious. Who knows what could have happened." He sipped his tea, his forehead wrinkled in a frown.

Mrs. Douglass waited for the right moment to say what was on her mind, but feared it would never come. Placing her cup on the desk she leaned toward her husband. "On Tuesday I went to the Family Guidance Centre."

He didn't try to hide his surprise.

"I know what you're thinking. We don't need strangers to help us bring up our daughter. But — well, I wondered if it would make a difference and I decided it couldn't do any harm. Martha's been taking Duncan there and she told me she felt it helped. She thought maybe Duncan was getting something out of it too."

"But that kid's got problems!"

"Yes, he has. And so has Elizabeth. They're not as drastic as his but they're problems just the same."

"All teenage girls have crushes that don't work out."

"That's not her problem and we both know it." She picked up her tea with a little laugh. "Poor Elizabeth's got two old fogies who didn't get to be parents until they were at an age when they should've been paying out their kid's university tuition. Most of our friends are becoming grandparents. We're way behind, Brian."

He had to smile too. Taking her hand in his he asked, "Did you realize it was going to be this much trouble, Sandra?"

"What parents actually think about the troubles? At least we're normal that way."

"So what did the family counsellor say?"

"Well, at first she just listened while I talked about the night of Elizabeth's birthday party and about Cass. Then she said that these things were just symptoms and asked when we first started to feel there was a problem.

"I wasn't sure what to say. I couldn't remember when it actually started. Then I found myself telling her all about how Elizabeth's grade one teacher wanted her to switch into grade two halfway through the year because she was so bright. I explained how worried we were about pushing Elizabeth too much and about her always being with older children. That's when she said something that really made me think, Brian. She said,

'So because Elizabeth accelerated, you and your husband tried to keep her from growing up ahead of her time.' "

Mrs. Douglass touched the handle of her teacup but didn't pick it up. "That's what we've been doing, isn't it, Brian?"

He shifted his weight in his chair and thought back to their decision to let Elizabeth move ahead to grade two. To skip a grade ahead of her little friends seemed a gigantic leap for their daughter to make. But they hadn't wanted to hold her back either.

"But now she's sneaking out of the house behind our backs," he said.

"It's all part of the same thing. She'll gain her freedom whatever way she can, with or without our permission."

"So what's the solution? Did the counsellor give you a magic answer?"

"Not really."

"Then what do we do next?"

"We have to start giving her some freedom and teach her how to use it. That's our role. Because if we keep refusing to loosen our ties she'll snap the rope on us and be gone."

"Counsellors are great at drawing pictures in words, aren't they?" he said with a smile. Then he sighed heavily.

"We have to try, Brian."

He tightened his fingers around her hand. Then he reached for more tea.

June 7

Getting dressed that morning had been an impossible task. Mrs. Douglass had taken out the sleeve seam of a blouse so it would fit over the bulky cast, but Elizabeth knew that it looked stupid.

Even before the bell rang for the first class there were lots of signatures on her cast. Woody had written: "Some people will do anything to get out of writing exams." Carolyn's note said: "Them's the breaks." Most of the other kids had just scrawled their names. She had drawn a large red heart near the wrist for Cass to write in.

She felt secure knowing there were only five people who knew the real truth about the accident: herself, Cass, Woody (who hadn't lectured her at all), Carolyn and Belinda. The secret was safe.

All the details had been worked out for the exams. She could take them orally rather than write them. The thought of spending two hours in a room with a teacher while she tried to think and talk at the same time was putting on the pressure.

How could you remember all the facts and organize them, the way you usually could, with a teacher sitting there the whole time staring you right in the face?

In the cafeteria it seemed as if no one had ever seen a cast before.

"This okay?" asked Carolyn, sliding the two trays onto a table.

"Sure."

"Hey, there's Paul. He's coming over."

"Oh, no," groaned Elizabeth.

"I heard all about it, Elizabeth," Paul beamed, putting down his lunch tray. "That's the biggest cast I ever saw."

"Thanks," she replied, struggling with her fork and jabbing it into the salad. If Paul really had heard it all he'd freak, she thought, smugly guarding her secret.

"So are your folks laying it on heavy? Bet there's not a chance they'll give you permission to take Cass to the grad now. Boy, they must be burned that you took off to Carolyn's."

"Paul," said Carolyn, "shut up."

Elizabeth speared a tomato slice on her fork. She had the urge to throw it at Paul but somehow held back.

"Geez, you guys are touchy. You'd think it was a big secret or something."

Carolyn changed the topic. "What about the graduation meeting? Is everyone going? We've got less than a week before that stuff's got to be ready to put up in the gym."

"A lot of use I'm going to be with this thing." Elizabeth lifted her arm and nearly knocked Paul right in the nose, not noticing that he was leaning to read what had been written on the cast.

"Hey, can I write on it?" he asked.

"Not now, I'm eating."

"You're not using this arm. Come on, Elizabeth, don't be such a pain."

With a heavy sigh she gave up as Paul dug into his backpack to get a pen.

She rolled her eyes. When she looked back at him, her face turned as white as her cast. Through the centre of the red heart she'd reserved for Cass, Paul had written his name.

"Are you crazy?" she asked hoarsely.

"Just a joke," he said, turning his pen over and using the eraser to rub out what he'd written. "Erasable ink, get it? Just testing your reflexes."

"Let's go to that meeting," said Elizabeth, pushing back her chair. "Someone get my tray, please."

"I will," said Paul enthusiastically, but Elizabeth didn't hear him as she turned to leave the cafeteria.

"Some joke," groaned Woody when Paul repeated the story to him in the halls.

"Everyone's too serious," Paul returned.

"But she knows you want to ask her to the grad. And she's touchy about that topic, to say the least." He remembered his own attempt to ask her.

"Who said anything about that to her?"

"A heart on a necklace as a birthday present speaks for itself."

"But no one said anything about asking her."

"Asking who about what?" said Carolyn, coming up behind them.

"Skip it," said Paul, and he went into the art room by himself.

"What's with him?"

"Paul wants to ask Elizabeth to the dance and she knows it. He probably thinks he's got a chance now that she's in trouble."

"Ohhh," said Carolyn, getting the entire picture.

When she and Woody walked into the art room it was clear that Paul was still trying. There he was, the same guy who had said he wasn't helping with the art work, standing next to the drawing of the Ferris wheel. He had a dripping red paintbrush in his hand. Elizabeth was doing her best to ignore him.

Woody sauntered over and pointed at the paintbrush. "I see you've decided to paint your way into Elizabeth's heart."

"Cut it out, Woody."

"Nothing's changed, you know. You won't be taking her to the dance."

"Neither will Cass." He smacked the oozing red brush against the paper spread out on the floor and began to colour in one of the Ferris wheel seats.

It was about ten minutes later that Woody looked up from his sketch of the tilt-a-whirl and saw Paul painting very close to where Elizabeth was working. This he had to see. He eased his way over to within earshot.

"Just give me a chance," Paul was saying.

"What's the good of getting mad even before I've said anything?"

"You don't take no for an answer, do you?"

"Face it, he isn't going to be allowed to go. What's there to lose if you go with me?"

"Cass and I are going steady."

"And Cass is off-limits to you. What about that little point?"

"Paul, I'm not going to the grad with you."

"Better me than no one."

"No, Paul. I said no!"

"Why don't you say yes but if Cass can take you — which I absolutely doubt — I'll let him."

Elizabeth's cheeks flushed red. Recognizing this sign of her temper, Woody backed away. Paul sure was a sucker for punishment.

June 8

Woody's smoking habit had been replaced by his Sonia habit, but kissing could only ease the pressure of exams so much. A cigarette was what he needed. Constantly. In his room he'd hung a poster which showed an ape sitting in a jail and smoking six cigarettes at once. There were times he envied that ape.

Exams were just a week away but it was Saturday. Nobody could study on a Saturday night, especially Woody. He'd taken Sonia to a movie that was supposed to be a good one. From what he saw of it he'd have to say it had potential. Now, having walked her home and said goodnight a hundred and eleven times, Woody headed for Frankie's Arcade to avoid going home to stare at boring TV.

Cass's bike was parked in its usual place in front of Frankie's.

As soon as Woody got his kneecaps inside the door Paul bolted toward him. "Guess who's here?"

"You?" What was it about Paul, especially lately,

that made you want to tell him to get lost, or at least fade into the background?

"Cass! And he's drunk!"

"So what? You never see a guy drunk before?"

"Just wait until you see him. He's really asking for it."

"Look, Paul, every time something happens that could get Cass and Elizabeth in more trouble you start acting like it's a holiday. Cut it out, why don't you? Give up."

"Why should I?"

"Oh, forget it."

By now he could see Cass and some of the guys he hung around with. Frankie was giving them a heart-to-heart. Woody casually walked over to see what was up.

"It's none of my business," Frankie was saying, "what you do outside my place. But you're in here and it *is* my business. None of you guys're in any shape to use these machines and I don't like having people in here in your condition. Now this is no big trip I'm laying. Glad to have you back tomorrow. Let's just stop things before they get a chance to start."

One of the guys started giving Frankie some mouth and that's when Cass spoke up. "He's just doing us a favour," he said. "That's all you're doin', ain't it, Frankie."

"Sure, Cass."

"Hear that? He's only doin' us a favour. Let's go while there's no trouble."

Woody figured Cass wasn't drinking that much

because his words were at least in recognizable sentence patterns.

"Hey, here's my friend Woody. How ya doin', Woody ol' buddy?"

"What's up, Cass?"

"Just leavin'. Me and the guys here've been partying. Elizabeth's grounded. How do you like that? On a Saturday night too. So I've been with these jerks." He laughed and slapped one of the guys on the shoulder. "You see Elizabeth today?"

"No."

"When you see her say hi, will ya, Woody? From me. Her parents've been watching her like a hawk. Two hawks." He laughed aloud, looking around at the other guys, but none of them got his joke.

"She's studying for exams, I guess," said Woody as a kind of excuse for Elizabeth's parents.

"Yeah. She's got a brain, that girl. Well, Frankie wants us to vacate, don't you, Frankie ol' buddy? He's right. See ya around, Woody. Say hi to Elizabeth, remember."

The guys piled out the door, stumbling and carrying on.

"Did Cass drive his bike here?" asked Woody, beginning to realize that the trouble might be just starting.

"No, it's been here for a couple of hours," said Frankie. "He was around earlier, then left for a while without taking the bike."

As if on cue, a police car cruised past the arcade and slowed down to see what all the commotion was about.

"Oh-oh," muttered Woody. "Better go see what happens."

Paul was right behind him.

The police parked the cruiser and one of them sauntered back to where the guys were still acting like idiots. Cass was sitting sideways against his bike as though he'd never think of driving it in a million years.

"What's up, gentlemen?" asked the police officer.

"Lovely night, officer," grinned one of the guys stupidly.

"Might be time for you boys to be home. Wouldn't want to see any trouble now, would we?"

"No way, officer. Not from us."

A couple of the guys shuffled their feet, anxiously looking around for some way out of the situation.

"No one's driving, I presume."

"No, sir. We're just walking," said the guy closest to the police officer, holding up his foot and losing his balance in a sideways step.

"And how about this bike?"

Cass pretended he didn't notice.

Woody decided he'd better say something, especially since Paul had just poked him in the ribs, figuring Cass would be arrested or something. "Sir, my name's Woody Harris. This bike doesn't belong to me. It belongs to my friend Cass here, but he just asked me in there if I'd drive it home for him tonight because . . . " His voice trailed off without stating the obvious, which just might be saying too much. So far this officer seemed to be trying to give them all a break.

"Well, that's very sensible of your friend. Do you have a licence?"

Woody took out his wallet and dug through it to find his driver's licence.

"Hmmm," murmured the officer, eyeing Woody and studying the licence.

"I'm just short," offered Woody when it looked as if the man didn't believe he was old enough to drive. Woody wished his licence didn't look so crisply new.

"Here's the keys, buddy," said Cass matter-of-factly, getting ready to settle on the back.

"Okay, then, how about the rest of you taking a free taxi-ride home? My constable friend and I can drop you off, no problem at all."

Since he said it as if they had no choice, the boys got very serious looks on their faces and allowed themselves to be herded into the car. They were squeezed in like mourners on the way to a funeral.

When the police car slowly pulled away, Cass sighed in relief. "Thanks. I owe you one."

"Forget it."

"Phew!" exclaimed Paul. "That would've really clinched it for you, Cass. Arrested!"

"What're you getting at?" Cass got off the bike and stood in front of Paul.

"You almost got arrested."

"What for?"

"Drinking and driving."

"Who's drinking and driving?" Cass was leaning closer to Paul but Paul wasn't getting the hint to shut up.

"You. If Woody hadn't said what he did you would've been arrested."

"Why don't you mind your own business? I'm not arrested, am I? The cops aren't here anymore, are they? So what's the big deal?"

Paul sneered. "Elizabeth sure is sucked in by you."

At the same instant that Woody was thinking he'd better interfere again, Cass's right hand, clenched into a fist, shot out and caught Paul square in the jaw. Paul stumbled backward about two and a half steps but he didn't fall. Shock was written all over his face, especially in that one small patch where a red glow was printed.

No one said anything.

Woody decided not to mention that Paul had it coming to him. And it looked like the fight was over before it really got started.

"Let's go, Cass." Woody got on the bike, putting on Elizabeth's purple helmet which Cass kept tied on the bike just in case. Cass got on too, sliding his leg over the seat, not once taking his eyes off Paul.

For once Paul kept his mouth shut. He'd have a bruise to explain, that was certain.

"Your place?" asked Woody.

"Yeah. I'll sneak in."

Woody enjoyed the chance to get behind the controls of the 750, but with Cass in his condition and trying to hold on to the chrome bar in back of him, Woody didn't exactly give the bike a workout. Enough close calls for one night, he thought.

"I'll walk back part way with you," said Cass,

crawling off the back of the bike and finding his centre of balance as he stood. "Mom's still up watching TV and she'll nail me if I go in like this. Some air'll do me good."

The blue light from a television flickered eerily in the living room window of Cass's house. Woody didn't figure that a walk would make the kind of difference Cass was picturing, but he couldn't see where it would hurt, either. "Sure. Let's go."

For early June it wasn't very warm, but it was nice out just the same. The light of the street lamps shone through the leafy trees that lined the boulevard. Things were really quiet at one in the morning. As they passed a neighbouring house a small dog bolted from the front porch, yapping and snarling until Cass called it by name and ordered it to go home and mind its own business. It did.

"D'you think Paul will tell Elizabeth I hit him?" Cass said.

"Yeah."

"Damn."

"Yeah."

Cass walked sideways into Woody, who had to steer him for a step or two.

"I dunno." Cass seemed to be doing a lot of thinking behind those two simple words.

"She won't pay much attention to Paul," said Woody.

"Maybe her parents are right." Cass stopped abruptly, as though he couldn't walk and think at the same time. "Besides, we don't even get to see each other now." He started to walk again. "And then there's university,"

"What about university?"

"I tried to talk to her about that last week but she didn't understand." Cass grabbed Woody's arm and stared closely into his face — too closely, since his breath smelled like a brewery. "My brother says university is more fun than work. Parties, roommates, basketball games. He's bustin' to get back there when the summer's over."

They started walking again.

"So what are you getting at?" asked Woody.

"Elizabeth says I'm wrong, but sooner or later she'll be having so much fun I'll fade right out of the picture." He stared ahead as if he'd only been talking to himself.

For Woody it seemed strange to be walking along hearing his footsteps mix with Cass's on the sidewalk in the empty darkness and listening to him describe what, very likely, would be true. What could he say?

"You going to university?" Cass asked. That last word had sounded like a mouthful of marbles.

"Yeah."

"What for? I mean, what're you going to be?"

"I dunno. A doctor maybe. If I can get good enough marks to get into medical school."

"A doctor. Phew," Cass whistled softly. "Money. Big money. Wouldn't want to cut people though." He hiccuped.

"Hold your breath and count to a hundred," Woody suggested.

Cass gulped in a mouthful of air and held it. Silence. Then he exhaled in a gasp. "You'd be a good doctor."

"I quit smoking." Suddenly Woody felt a bit foolish blurting that out, like it gave him some kind of right to be a doctor just because he was trying to kick the smoking habit.

"Good idea. Doctors'd look stupid smoking. Like guys who work with dynamite. Boooom!"

They both broke up laughing and their voices echoed along the street.

"Hey! My hiccups're gone! Thanks."

"I'll send you a bill."

"Guess I'll cut back now," said Cass when they got to the main intersection. "Maybe I'll phone Elizabeth. I dunno though. Maybe not. Might start a scene with her parents."

"They're not bad really," said Woody.

"No. Probably do the same thing myself if I had a daughter like Elizabeth and she was going with a guy like me. They want to make sure she does all right."

"You're all right."

"But I mean with university and doing something with those brains of hers." Then he added, "She'll probably phone me up. She does all the time."

Woody started across the street as the light turned green.

"Thanks for the favour!" yelled Cass.

"Forget it!"

Woody continued alone to his place. All this fuss

Elizabeth's going through about Cass, he thought, and by next year this time maybe they won't even be what you'd call friends. It wasn't likely that Cass would wait around to be a once-in-a-while boyfriend. And with Elizabeth being so gorgeous it wasn't likely the guys at university would ignore her.

Meanwhile graduation was right after exams, and for Elizabeth and Cass it didn't look like it'd be a night to celebrate much.

June 9

Woody felt like he was still sleeping but that was impossible because he could smell bacon and coffee. And his mother was walking in front of him saying something about Elizabeth on the phone sounding very excited.

"Excited good or excited bad?" said Woody to the back of his mother's pink satin housecoat as his brain emerged from the dusty corridors of his dreaming.

"Hello," he said.

"Woody! It's me, Elizabeth! I know I woke you up but I had to tell you."

Paul couldn't have blabbed the gossip about the fight and Cass's drinking this early on a Sunday morning, he thought. But knowing Paul . . .

"I was awake, sort of. Kind of like I never really got to sleep if you know what I mean." He knew he was stalling, trying to figure a way to play down Paul's story, but so far his brain was still only half awake.

"Guess what?"

"What?" He braced himself for the worst.

"Mom and Dad say I can take Cass to the graduation dance!"

Stunned by the complete surprise of this statement, Woody could only manage a kind of grunt. "Huh?"

"You heard me right. Isn't that terrific? Oh, Woody, I can hardly believe it myself. I've already called Cass and he thinks they've flipped, but they haven't. They really did say it! Carolyn and I are going to shop for my dress tomorrow right after school. She says I'll have to wear one with little shoe-string straps because of this cast and maybe I'll get a flimsy shawl to sort of cover up and — "

"Hold it!" Woody practically yelled into the phone. She was spilling everything out too fast.

Elizabeth laughed. "I'm so happy!"

"Well — but — " Whether it was because he'd been up until he couldn't drag one more movie out of the television or because he hadn't had a single cigarette in weeks, Woody couldn't get a sentence from his brain cells to the tip of his tongue.

"I know. I know," Elizabeth said. "It's too much to believe, isn't it? Well, something happened last night that changed everything."

One thing for sure, Woody knew, Paul hadn't had a chance to tell his big news.

"Dad and Mom went to dinner at someone's house — I think a guy Dad works with. Anyway, guess who was there?"

"Cass?"

"No, dummy. Mr. MacClaren."

"The principal?"

"Just listen. Mr. MacClaren got talking about our graduation and things and all about me, I guess — that's what Mom said. He told Mom and Dad that he thought I was a good student and that he and the other teachers had great hopes for my future because I was going to such a good university and that he felt I was showing leadership with the graduation committee — things like that. Anyway, by the time he finished talking I guess Mom and Dad started doing some thinking. Mom said they talked for hours in bed after they got home. And by the time they went to sleep they'd decided that maybe I was responsible enough to take Cass to the graduation dance and it wouldn't be the end of the world or anything! Can you believe it!"

Now it was all beginning to make sense.

"That's great news, Elizabeth. It sure is great news."

"And that's not all. Dad even said Cass could drive our car so we can go someplace after the dance. I could tell it's because he doesn't want me to go on Cass's bike or in some old wreck but who cares, we've got wheels! And I was just talking to Carolyn and she said she and Mark would go with us, and you and Sonia should come too. It'll be great!"

"Better get the car thing in writing before your father regains consciousness. Who knows what they were serving for cocktails at that dinner party."

"Isn't it fantastic? Listen, Woody, I gotta go."

She stopped to catch her breath, which made him grin. Things sure could change in a flash.

"I'll see you in school or on the way or something. Anyway, bye. I'm going to have a heart attack."

As soon as he hung up the phone a picture flashed through Woody's mind of Paul with his jaw turning bright red, staring speechless at Cass. If Paul got to Elizabeth before Woody got to Paul, all her excitement about graduation would go right down the drain.

He grabbed the phone and took it into the hall closet, shutting the door. He didn't want anyone to hear what he was about to say to Paul, especially his mother who was right around the corner in the kitchen frying bacon. In the darkness, amid coats and sneakers, Woody carefully dialled Paul's number.

"Good morning, Mrs. Blackburn. This is Woody Harris. I'm in Paul's chemistry class at school. I know it's early in the morning but could you possibly wake Paul up? I'm stuck on this equation I'm working through and it's driving me nuts. I just have to ask Paul for some help. He's so good at chemistry." Mothers always liked to hear compliments about their sons.

While he waited in the darkness Woody formulated an equation of a different sort: Paul's big mouth plus anything said about last night equalled an unrecognizable face. Or maybe instead of threats, sheer pleading would be the answer. The guy must realize he'd lost the chance with Elizabeth by now. But he wouldn't put it past Paul to want to get in one last punch.

"Harris, is this some kind of joke? It's barely daylight. What're you feeding Mom about chemistry help?"

Woody decided it wasn't good tactics to plead with a guy you'd just awakened out of a Sunday morning sleep-in. "Look, Paul, this is drastic. I mean it. If you don't listen to me and do exactly what I tell you, I'll — I don't know what I'll do. But it'll be big."

"What are you talking about? What did you do last night? Where are you?"

"I'm home. And I didn't do anything last night except drive Cass to his place and walk home. But it's last night I want to talk to you about. What does your face look like this morning?"

"Pretty normal. I checked before I came downstairs. There's a sort of mark but it's not swollen much. I've got a feeling if I don't shave today no one'll know."

"Wait a minute," said Woody, trying to put together what Paul was saying. "Do you mean you don't want people to know that Cass hit you?"

"Are you crazy? I'd never hear the end of that. I didn't even get a punch in. I'd look like an idiot. Listen, Woody, I know you're mad at me for bugging Elizabeth and all that, and I wouldn't blame you if you told her I'd been flattened by Cass, but — well, would you do me a favour and not mention it? I know I'd owe you one but — "

"Say no more, Paul. My mouth is a time capsule

set to go off in the year six trillion. Elizabeth will never know."

"Thanks, Woody."

"Okay. So long then."

"Hey, Woody?"

"Yeah?"

"Why did you call really? Mom said something about chemistry, then you start talking about what my face looks like and — "

"Oh. Well, I called because — Uh, because I didn't know if your parents knew you'd got punched and — well, they might've wondered and — Uh, maybe I could've helped you make up some kind of excuse or something."

"You'd do that for me? Really, Woody?"

"Sure, why not?"

"Well, you know — I guess I did a few dumb things."

"Forget it."

"And listen. I decided not to try to ask Elizabeth to graduation. I'm asking this girl I know from over where my grandmother has a cottage. I saw her there last weekend and I got thinking about it."

"Good idea. Ask her today."

"Yeah."

"And about Elizabeth," Woody added. "Her father gave her permission to take Cass to the dance. He's even giving them the car."

Paul's silence said it all.

"See you at school," Woody said. He hung up and squeezed out of the closet. His mother's eyebrows lifted in an obvious question. He decided the best thing was to ignore it, and he turned and went back up the stairs yawning and saying something about catching up on his sleep.

Hard to believe, he thought as he crawled back between the rumpled sheets, but things were falling into place. Cass was taking Elizabeth to the grad against all odds. Sonia was anxious to be his date. And Paul was out of the way. It was like snapping the last scattered pieces of a jigsaw puzzle into position.

June 26

On the morning of graduation it was pouring rain. Carolyn telephoned Elizabeth, upset because they were supposed to be going to get their hair done at one o'clock. And how could they possibly look good wearing rain jackets to their graduation?

"It'll stop," said Elizabeth. There wasn't a single solitary thing that could prevent graduation day from being an absolutely perfect one.

But at ten to one the sky opened up and it poured as they raced from the bus stop. Carolyn and Elizabeth looked like two survivors of a boating accident when they entered the hairdresser's.

"How'll we ever get home without ruining our hair?" Carolyn asked.

But by the time they were finished the sun had squeezed its way through the heavy grey clouds and the last insistent raindrops were falling intermittently.

"Hey," said Elizabeth as they walked out into the sunlight, "everything's just been cleaned up for graduation." She took a deep breath and unzipped her rain jacket. "This is a perfect day."

Cass arrived right on time. He looked a bit strange wearing his silver and red helmet with a tuxedo, especially with a velvet bow tie under his chin.

"Here he is," Elizabeth's father said as he pushed aside the living room drapes. "Prince Charming arriving on his steed."

A lot of pictures were taken — Elizabeth and Cass standing in front of the fireplace, then sitting on the sofa, Elizabeth in the large armchair with Cass behind her, and the two of them waving goodbye as they started down the walkway toward the car.

Elizabeth's dress, with its pattern of small meadow flowers in pastel blue, yellow and pink on white, fluttered in the June breeze. The delicate blue shawl she wore partially hid her bulky cast. Cass had brought a corsage of five tiny yellow roses and she was wearing it on the wrist that wasn't buried under white plaster-of-Paris.

After closing the car door for Elizabeth, Cass strode around to the driver's seat, adjusting his bow tie and nervously smiling at Mr. Douglass, who watched from the front door. "You can take the 750 for a ride if you want, sir!" he shouted.

Mrs. Douglass was laughing and nodding "yes" behind her husband's back as Cass slowly backed out of the driveway. Then he drove away in a performance any dad would be proud of, especially the dad who owned the car.

They stopped at Woody's house and Elizabeth had to get out while Mrs. Harris took a picture of her and Woody standing on the front lawn.

"Here you are graduating from high school when it seems like only yesterday I was taking a picture of you two with your new school bags over your shoulders heading off to school for the first time."

"Just take the picture, Mom," said Woody. "You'll get Elizabeth crying and all that blue stuff around her eyes will slide down her face. And make sure the sun's not reflecting on my glasses. For once I'd like a picture where I don't have laserbeam eyes."

"Straighten your cummerbund, Woody," said his mother from behind the camera.

Finally the pictures were taken, kisses were lightly planted on cheeks and the three were ready to proceed to Carolyn's house. Sonia's would be the last stop.

"Phew!" whistled Cass as he pulled the car into the circular driveway in front of Sonia's house. "This place is a country club."

"But Sonia's not a snob," said Woody, getting out of the back seat with an orchid carefully held in a plastic box.

"Let's move over, Mark, to make room for the two of them," suggested Carolyn, adjusting her yellow dress to avoid wrinkles.

Elizabeth tried to straighten Cass's bow tie, which was tilting stubbornly. "There, that should stay now." But it didn't.

Sonia's mother was fussing with her daughter's

hair, which had been gathered in a small cluster of braids at the crown of her head. In her blue silk dress Sonia seemed much older than she really was, and Woody beamed proudly beside her as they came down the steps to the car. The orchid looked perfect.

Before Woody could reach for the back door to open it for her she had quickly slipped into the front seat beside Elizabeth, saying something about how crowded they'd all be in the back together and how their dresses would look a mess by the time they got to school.

Sullenly, but trying to accept Sonia's explanation, Woody made some introductions.

"We have to get ready for the procession," Elizabeth said to Cass as he locked the car. "Why don't you and Sonia go into the auditorium and find somewhere to sit? Mom and Dad'll be here soon. Save them a seat."

"Good idea," agreed Woody. "And save space for my folks too. They're driving Elizabeth's parents."

Sonia smiled too sweetly at Cass, thought Woody. She sure was acting funny.

"As soon as the ceremony is over we'll meet at the reception, okay?" Elizabeth said.

"Sure," replied Cass, finally letting go of her hand.

"Doesn't Sonia look beautiful? And the orchid is perfect!" Woody followed Elizabeth down the hall. He knew he sounded like a babbling idiot but the words tumbled out nervously.

"You look pretty great yourself," said Elizabeth

with a grin, taking his hand as they rushed to the AV room.

Miss Johnston was lining everyone up in alphabetical order, as if they'd all graduated from her English class without knowing the alphabet. Elizabeth was only seven people ahead of Woody.

Mr. MacClaren, the principal, came into the room to smile officiously at everyone. He straightened a couple of ties, then stopped by Elizabeth and said, "We're proud of you tonight, young lady. Quite proud."

He cleared his throat for attention and said loudly, "I don't know where the boys and girls I pass in the halls every day have gone tonight, but they've been replaced by a fine gathering of young ladies and gentlemen."

He surveyed the group as they nervously stared at fingernails or checked their zippers and buttons. "Of course I will have a chance to congratulate you all individually as you come up to receive your certificates. Remember, Thackery, shake with the right and take with the left." That made everyone crack up because he'd kept saying that at the rehearsal the day before.

MacClaren calmed everyone down with another loud *ahem,* then continued what he'd started to say. "But, while you're all here together I want to say that we have a particularly fine group of graduates this year — people who've excelled, people who've made plans to attend our country's best universities, and people who, although they've not yet made clear plans for their futures, will steer and direct their lives in most interesting and productive ways. You're no longer children. You're men and women."

When the principal left the room Woody sneaked up to Elizabeth and asked, "What did he say to you before he gave us that kiss-off speech?"

"It was strange. Something about being proud of me. Wonder what it was all about?"

"Dunno," said Woody, but he was thinking they'd soon find out.

"Mr. Harris, H does not come directly after D," said Miss Johnston, not really able to cut the sarcasm even on graduation night.

Just as Woody got back to his place the music started and the line began its slow procession into the auditorium. The only person Woody wanted to see was Sonia, and he did. But she didn't see him because she was busy whispering something to Cass, who was grinning and waving at Elizabeth. His parents and the Douglasses were there too.

Graduations were long ceremonies. Woody had forgotten that. It wasn't exactly boring, just long.

Elizabeth was thinking about how her parents were back there sitting next to Cass. After all this time, there they were. It was worth all the trouble. And she was thinking about coming home next year and inviting Cass for dinner at their place and telling everyone stories about university.

The valedictorian had chosen to talk about life being like a small brook growing into a stream and then into a river and finally flowing into the sea. A bit of a tired theme, thought Woody, but it was a good one to get the parents feeling mellow.

It was funny, he thought, because he couldn't picture himself just flowing passively along until his life had blended into the ocean of all humanity. Maybe that's not quite what the valedictorian had in mind, but sitting there on that uncomfortable steel chair he knew he wanted a life that was more unique than that. Maybe he'd be a surgeon who could implant bionic parts to extend the lives of terminal patients. Or something else that was different. Not just looking into ears and throats and telling patients to lose weight and quit smoking.

Finally Mr. MacClaren stood up to give the academic awards. In a flash of insight, just as the principal opened his folder there at the podium, Woody knew what he had meant when he'd told Elizabeth earlier that they were proud of her. She was getting a scholarship! He just knew it!

"Psssst!" whispered Woody, leaning to catch Elizabeth's eye. When she looked at him he raised his hand, making an okay *O* with his thumb and finger. It made him laugh smugly when she just looked at him in confusion.

MacClaren really knew how to lay it on. Any minute now he'd probably mention all the world leaders and how pleased they were to learn about the top scholarship winner. And it was a big deal, nobody could say it wasn't.

When the principal finally got to the part where he was going to give the winner's name Woody stopped watching him and looked over at Elizabeth to see the expression that was soon going to burst on her face.

"Elizabeth Margaret Douglass."

Her mouth dropped open but she didn't move and she didn't say a word. People beside her were poking her and grabbing her hand and laughing, while the whole auditorium exploded with clapping.

Then the truth sank in and she eased her way along the row to the centre aisle. As she passed in front of Woody he took her hand and kissed it grandly, like he was Prince Charming and she was Her Royal Highness of Somewhere, just up the street.

"I'm going to cry," she said.

"Think of your mascara," he said with a chuckle to try to make things easier.

"Four thousand dollars a year for each of four years," Mr. MacClaren announced. "Of course the monetary value is only a small portion of the great significance this has for Elizabeth's education. She has been recognized both academically and personally by one of the most prestigious universities of our country. Elizabeth, we are all very proud of you tonight." And he gave her a kiss on the cheek while Miss Johnston fluttered around just behind him waiting for her turn to beam at this year's top academic winner.

Woody didn't need to look back to know that Mrs. Douglass was probably crying. Maybe his mother was too. And Mr. Douglass would be grinning. When he thought of Cass, Woody had a feeling that he was proud too, but a bit nervous about what a four thousand dollar scholarship winner would be like when she came home to visit from university.

The ceremony proceeded from the awarding of prizes to the giving out of certificates. Woody straightened in his seat and pushed his glasses up farther on his nose. He knew, because the exams hadn't been so bad, that his marks would be good. But the question was whether or not they'd be good enough to get him any kind of consideration for medical school. The career counsellor had said about a dozen times that the admissions board at medical school looked at high school results, especially in the sciences, as well as marks from the three years of pre-med. The chemistry exam had been a killer.

At last Woody was ready to go on stage. A camera flashed as his certificate was presented.

Then he was back in his seat. He slid the ribbon from around the certificate and unfurled it. Quickly his eyes darted to the list of marks — 79, 80, 81, 76, down and down the list until he saw chemistry. 84. Honours! He'd actually pulled off an honours in chemistry! Maybe the other marks weren't so outstanding, he thought with a grin, but that 84 would blind the medical school admissions board. And he had three years of pre-med to pour into the books and come up with more marks that were dazzlers. Doctor W. Harris!

No one could get near Elizabeth at the reception. Parents, students and teachers were all pressing close, holding their coffee or punch and trying to shake hands with her or give her a congratulatory kiss. So Woody went over to Cass, a bit surprised not to find Sonia there.

"Medical school next stop," said Cass, shaking Woody's hand.

"Not quite but it's getting closer." Then Woody's smile faded. "Where's Sonia?"

"She was here a minute ago," said Cass. But he wasn't really paying much attention. He was waiting for the mob to clear around Elizabeth.

Woody still couldn't find Sonia, even after he'd shaken hands with Mr. Douglass. He proudly deposited his certificate with his mother, who didn't make matters any better when she asked him where the "little girl" was that he'd brought to the graduation.

Pushing through the crowd he searched for that distinctive coal-black hair tied up in braids. Then he found her. She was up on her tiptoes giving a congratulatory kiss to one of the tallest players on the basketball team. Not on the cheek either, he noted jealously. When Woody finally got over to them the guy was wiping cinnamon lipstick from his mouth with the back of his hand.

"There you are," said Woody, trying to sound cheerful and not like a jealous madman with a blade of steel hidden under his tuxedo.

"Hi, guy," boomed the basketball player. "Like that red tie. Class. Real class."

"Yeah. Thanks. Hey, Sonia, I want you to meet my folks, okay?"

"Hey, are you two together?" asked the giant, pinching the end of his chin so he could think better.

"Yeah," said Woody.

Sonia was gazing at the basketball player.

"Geez. Well, we'll see ya then." And he sauntered off, trying to keep his elbows out of people's faces.

"Did you see his date?" asked Sonia as she and Woody headed back to meet his parents.

"Probably didn't have one. Maybe he doesn't like dances — that kind of desecration of the gym makes him shrink to normal size probably." He steered her to where his mom and dad stood waiting.

Most of the parents and relatives had left the reception by nine-thirty and the gym was cleared for the dance. Lights were turned off, except for some blue and yellow and red ones the band had rigged up. In that dimmed atmosphere the carousel carnival decorations took on a timeless quality. Looking up at the cotton candy cones he, Elizabeth and Carolyn had made, Woody had to admit that they actually looked like the real thing. He decided he'd get one for Sonia before the end of the dance.

"Hey, Woody, come help set up," shouted Mark. He and Carolyn were lugging a round table to the side of the gym.

"Sure," said Woody. "Carolyn, you and Sonia sit here. You can't move tables wearing those shoes and dresses."

Carolyn gave him one of her disgusted looks,

which said it all. "And you can't move anything wearing a red bow tie either," she replied sarcastically.

Sonia sat at the table as soon as Mark had spread the white cloth on it. Woody put a miniature graduation cap in the middle of the table and scattered a bit of confetti. Sonia stared at her shoulder straps and touched her braided hair lightly.

Wow, she's beautiful, thought Woody as he and Carolyn lifted more furniture into place.

The first twangs of electric guitars tuning up brought the rest of the people from the reception room into the gym.

Some of the graduates had come without dates. Not many but some. One of these singles was the basketball player, Woody noted without enthusiasm. How could he help but notice? That's where Sonia's eyes were glued practically the whole time.

When Woody took her hand she turned to smile sweetly but briefly at him. It wasn't quite the same, he thought, as being in her father's den pretending to study history.

"Let's go for a walk," she said in a polite voice.

Woody had noted the absence of the jolly green giant and put two and two together to figure out Sonia's real reason for wanting to go for a walk.

As they went outside the first person they saw was Paul with his date. This must be the girl from near his grandmother's cottage, Woody thought.

"Hey, I'd like you to meet Barbara San — "

But Paul was cut off in mid-sentence because

Woody had started after Sonia. She was already over by the basketball player. Paul got the picture.

After a few awkward moments standing around with the giant and Sonia while they were talking, Woody made a decision. For sure he didn't feel like hanging around here. He had nothing to say to this basketball player and he had his doubts about Sonia.

"Do you want to go back to the dance?" It was more a demand than a question. He was feeling set up before the set-up actually took place.

"No, not yet." She smiled at him, leaning toward the giant.

"Well, I'll see you in there maybe," said Woody and he turned and walked slowly away, stopping to introduce himself to Paul's date and then to shake hands with his chemistry teacher.

Elizabeth, Cass and Carolyn were sitting at the table. Cass's bow tie was lying beside Elizabeth's small purse. Mark was just coming along with four glasses of punch.

"Where's the crystal princess?" asked Mark as he set the paper cups on the table.

The other three stared at Woody for an answer.

"Making a pass at a guy on stilts."

"Are you serious?" asked Elizabeth, but he could see that she wasn't surprised about what was going on.

"If I'm right, that's the real reason she asked me to bring her here anyway. Probably didn't have the nerve to ask him, so she wangled a way to the dance where she could work her spell on him."

No one said anything.

"It worked," he added.

"That — " started Elizabeth angrily.

"Don't bother saying it," Woody said.

"Hi, you guys." It was Paul, not looking exactly easy at the idea of seeing Cass again. They hadn't laid eyes on each other since that night outside Frankie's.

But it was graduation. Everyone seemed in the mood to stop looking backwards and just look ahead. Cass pulled up an extra chair and Paul and Barbara sat down, with introductions all around. They all tried to pretend they didn't notice Sonia was missing. Even Paul managed to hold back any comments for once.

Then the band played a slow dance. There was Woody, deserted and alone at the table. Everyone else was dancing. High-heeled shoes were scattered here and there on the floor as girls danced in their stocking feet.

At least there was one good thing about the situation — Sonia didn't show up dancing with her nose pressed into the giant's tie clip. Woody sat there trying to look like a guy who just dropped by on his way to somewhere else. He had a melancholy thought about how fast the bliss of the past few weeks had burnt out. A couple of times he danced with girls that other guys had brought. The band was good. But he kept shooting a glance at the door to watch for Sonia to make an entrance with her hero. They didn't show.

"Think I'll go for a smoke," said Cass.

"Let me know if you see Sonia," Woody said.

"Should I say anything to her?"

"Nah. I'm just wondering if she's still around."

As Cass walked away Elizabeth turned to Woody with an exasperated look. "You're making this too easy for her. Why don't you go right out there — "

"And order her back in here to dance with me and be polite until I take her home and find the basketball hero waiting on her doorstep?"

"But — "

"Elizabeth, you once told me to save my advice. Right now I'm doing what I want to do. And I'm thinking about it."

"Okay. Okay." She got up and slipped her blue silk shawl off her shoulders. "Dance with me and my plaster-of-Paris friend here then."

The lights went out all at once and an explosive flash zapped like a laser beam from behind the drummer into the crowd. The two electric guitars growled and screamed in an extended, frenetic note while the drummer produced a succession of booming earthquake sounds. The red, blue and yellow lights suddenly began to flash rhythmically.

Elizabeth stood still in the middle of the gym floor, her head back, staring at the lights overhead. Then she began to move, just her shoulders at first and then her hips. She dropped her head forward so that her hair tumbled like a screen in front of her.

Woody gave a loud yelp that was drowned in the echo of guitars, and he was lost in the music.

Around him the carnival painted on the wall seemed to become animated, as though the music had breathed life into the flat shapes. Carousel horses grinned with open mouths. The Ferris wheel appeared to slide forward, down and then up, with the fiery red seats tilting and rocking. The roller coaster dipped and climbed along the wall. If Woody squinted his eyes almost shut, the gymnasium became a pulsing, electric carnival.

"I saw Sonia," announced Cass when the music finally stopped and they got back to their table.

"Back to reality," sighed Woody.

"She said to tell you she had to go home because she didn't feel well." Cass managed to say it without a hint of sarcasm in his voice.

"I think she didn't feel well when we picked her up." Woody didn't even try to hide his own sarcasm.

"I don't know why you asked her anyway," said Paul, right on cue.

"It's her lips, Paul," Woody said dramatically. "Ah, if you only knew those lips!"

"Guess that basketball player will get a chance to know."

"Paul," Cass said slowly, "do you have a short memory?" He curled his fist and tapped it into his palm.

Immediately the message got through.

"It's no big deal, Cass," said Woody.

"Is there something I don't know about?" asked Elizabeth, eyeing Cass's fist and noticing Paul shrinking back in his chair.

"No," replied Paul and Cass in unison.

"I think I won't ask any more questions," she muttered.

"Let's dance, Barbara," urged Paul, getting up and leading her away from the table.

"Hey," said Elizabeth, "we were talking about leaving soon to go change and then drive to the beach for a bonfire and some hot dogs. We're going to watch the sunrise. Come with us, Woody. You don't need a date."

He stretched and smiled through a yawn. "Guess it never stopped me before."

"I know what," said Cass enthusiastically. "If you want to, you can get my bike at Elizabeth's and drive out on that."

Woody thought of the 750 and getting a chance to drive it on the highway, heading to the beach by himself. No ties. No phoney anything. "You're on, Cass. Let's go!"

In Elizabeth's driveway Cass gave Woody a few last-minute tips he didn't really need. But he let Cass explain anyway.

"And you can wear my helmet," said Elizabeth, handing it to him. "Wait till we change. Then follow us."

"Nah, think I'll just head out. Meet you there." He fastened the strap of the purple helmet under his chin and straightened his red bow tie.

"Aren't you going to change?"

"Are you kidding? D'you know what this tux cost? I'm getting Mom's money's worth." He gave a kick, then another and another. The fourth kick jerked the Honda to a start and Woody grinned, revving the gas. "Where are you guys going exactly? Flat Rock Cove?" he shouted.

"Yeah. In about twenty minutes. See you there."

In the deserted night street Woody made the bike waltz back and forth as he drove away leaving Mark, Carolyn, Cass and Elizabeth laughing behind him. They watched his tuxedo flap in the breeze as the streetlights glinted off the helmet and the windshield and the chrome of the polished bike.

June 27

When the car arrived at Flat Rock Cove and Cass directed its lights down the beach they could see that Woody had not yet arrived.

"He's just having a ride," said Cass. "Let's get the fire started and make some hot dogs. I'm starving."

It was an almost ink-black night. There was only a quarter moon but millions of stars twinkled in the sky.

Mark had eaten six hot dogs and was contemplating roasting a seventh, Cass and Elizabeth were curled up in a blanket staring into the fire, and Carolyn was down at the water's edge wading into the black waves when they all heard Cass's bike growling up the beach road. Then they saw the light bobbing as the bike took the bumps and ruts.

Woody drove down onto the beach and raced toward them, passing the fire with a Tarzan shout. Slowing down, he turned back and stopped beside them.

"Did you start the sunrise without me?" he asked, sliding off the bike and pulling the purple helmet off.

"You're just in time," said Carolyn. "Isn't that blue over there, just at the very edge of the horizon?"

"Hot dog?" asked Mark.

"How'd you like the machine?" Cass sat up with one arm still stretched behind Elizabeth.

"Freedom. That's the word for it," Woody answered. "I'd love a hot dog. You cooking?"

"Where did you go?" asked Elizabeth.

"Nowhere. Everywhere. It's like your own world, isn't it?" he continued, stuffing a hot dog into his mouth.

"I like the wind," said Elizabeth.

"Yeah. And the noise from the bike makes a kind of silent universe inside the helmet. Know what I mean? I'm going to buy one of these machines," Woody declared.

Then Carolyn got to the point almost everyone was thinking about. "Are you okay? I mean about Sonia and all that?"

"Sure." He slopped some ketchup on another hot dog.

"Women!" said Mark, which brought a groan from Carolyn and Elizabeth.

"Pink! There it is! The sunrise!" announced Carolyn as if she were the official commentator. "I don't know if I ever really watched an entire sunrise. At least not after being up all night."

The blue was fading as pink spilled over the

horizon, catching the one single cloud that drifted at the edge of the ocean. They could see some ducks now, bobbing on the waves.

Elizabeth started to clap and they all joined in, cheering.

Soon the entire beach was bathed in early morning light and the ocean became its usual blue. A couple of seagulls swooped near the water's edge to catch breakfast by surprise.

Woody threw another piece of driftwood on the fire, sparks threading skyward.

Cass went back to the car saying there was something he'd forgotten. Mark and Carolyn strolled down to wade in the water. Curling the blanket to her chin, Elizabeth watched Woody stare into the flames.

"Are you sure you're okay?" she asked.

"Really sure." He turned toward her and gave a small grin. "It wasn't important. Like some things are and some things aren't."

"It was still a dirty thing to do to a person."

"Can't say it wasn't."

"I'd like to tell Sonia just what I think of her!"

"Wouldn't be worth it," said Woody. "Besides, I guess I knew all along that there was something behind all that attention. But I sort of decided I'd just enjoy it while it lasted. And I did."

"Woody, what is it about you that makes other people take advantage of you, people like Sonia?"

"What is it about other people that makes them take advantage of me?" He gave Elizabeth a quick glance and then leaned to pick up a handful of sand.

"You mean me, don't you?"

"I mean anyone." He let the sand slide in a stream from one palm to the other, captured and recaptured.

She sighed and pulled the blanket more securely around her. "You're thinking about the night of the movie. And the night Duncan — "

"Threw up," Woody finished for her and he burst out laughing. "What's all this serious stuff anyway, Elizabeth? It's grad night. Cut the serious stuff, okay?"

"It didn't seem wrong asking you to pretend we were going to the movie or to help with Duncan. Not like what Sonia did."

"It wasn't. Forget it."

"You were mad at me though."

"I was just mad that you made me part of a conspiracy against your parents."

"It was not a conspiracy!"

"Look, let's just drop this. It's grad night."

For a moment they both sat watching the fire. They could hear Carolyn's shouts as Mark pretended to splash her.

"Besides, I did try to talk to them. That night with Duncan. You were right there. And Dad just wouldn't — "

"You would have covered up that night too, somehow," interrupted Woody. "But you got caught. You had no way out." He wasn't in the mood to get into a heavy conversation with Elizabeth but there they were up to their knees in it. "Do you want to know what I think?" At least he'd give her the chance to shut him up.

"Sure, why not?"

No turning back now, he thought. "I figure you should still try to be straight with your folks."

"About what?"

"Everything. The movie night, the accident. Everything."

"Are you crazy? Why bring up stuff that's over with? What good would that do?"

"It would just clear up old business, you might say." But he could tell from the look on her face that she didn't even begin to agree. "Or you can do like you always do — just let everything slide. Then you can go to university and soon it will all be ancient history."

"But they're letting me be with Cass now."

"Yeah. But that's because MacClaren raved about you at that dinner party. It isn't really anything you did to change what your parents think. Besides, MacClaren just told about how you are in school."

"I'm not so different out of school."

"Then tell them what's been going on. Let them in on the whole truth. They might listen better now."

"I still don't see why I should bother. Me and Cass — "

"Is that all that matters to you? Cass and you? Your parents will be around a lot longer than — " He stopped himself in mid-sentence, then dropped the sand.

"Than what?" Her eyes challenged Woody.

But he didn't reply. Just because he figured Elizabeth and Cass wouldn't last much after she went to university was no reason to make her believe it, especially after all the hassle she'd just gone through about getting to the grad dance with him. "Nothing. It was just a dumb idea. Really. And here comes Cass. Let's just drop it, eh? It's grad night." He gave a small smile.

"Hey, Woody," said Cass as he approached the fire, "wanna try one of these to celebrate?" He held a couple of fat cigars.

"No, thanks," said Woody. "Too early in the morning for me. Or too late at night," he added, laughing.

"Suit yourself."

Elizabeth picked up a stick and poked at the embers of the fire. She wasn't smiling.

"If it's okay with you, Cass, now that I've seen the sun's performance I think I'll take another little ride. Shall I drop your bike at Elizabeth's or at your place?"

"Elizabeth's."

"Okay. See you guys. Hey, Mark! Carolyn!" he shouted. "I'm going! See you tomorrow somewhere!"

"See ya, Woody!"

"Thanks for the bike, Cass."

"No problem."

"Talk to you later, Elizabeth."

"Sure," she said, looking up at him and managing a half smile.

Graduation night was over. The sun had climbed

full and round up past the horizon, streaking golden light through the trees and off the tips of waves that rolled to shore. And it did feel different, Woody realized, knowing that he wouldn't be going back to the same tired building in the fall and that he wouldn't be in grade anything. He felt a lot older than just the night before. Or maybe it wasn't age. Maybe it was freedom.

When he came to the turnoff for the main highway into town Woody slowed Cass's Honda and began to make a left. But then he stopped. Why bother taking the fast route home? The old road had dips and curves and fantastic scenery along the ocean. Like in the poem about the two roads in the woods, he thought. Johnston had force-fed that poem to them and he could remember the last two lines being something about how the guy took the road that wasn't used much and that made a big difference.

That morning, after graduation, Woody felt in the mood to be different too. He leaned the bike to the right and pointed it in the direction of the old seaside highway.

Carolyn was sleeping against Mark's shoulder in the back seat and Cass held Elizabeth's hand as he drove slowly back to town. No one seemed in a hurry to get home.

"Why don't we stop somewhere for breakfast?" asked Cass.

"Burger, fries and a milkshake," agreed Mark from the back seat.

"Ugh, at breakfast?" said Elizabeth with disgust.

"Breakfast?" murmured Carolyn, stirring from sleep.

"Then we all agree," said Cass.

"I guess Dad can do without his car for another hour."

After they dropped Mark and Carolyn off, Cass and Elizabeth headed back home. Cass stretched his arm around Elizabeth and she leaned against his shoulder. She still wore the corsage of five yellow roses but now it was on her grey sweatshirt instead of her wrist. She buried her nose in the fading petals. "I guess graduation's definitely over. These flowers have had it."

Cass planted a kiss on her hair. "It was one of the best graduations I've been to."

"The only one," she teased.

"How does it feel to be a star? Four thousand dollars! Phew! That's a lot of dough."

"It's all like a dream. And I'm not even sure what I want to be — as a career, I mean."

"What about being a lawyer? Isn't that what you want to be?"

"A judge."

"Yeah. Well, that's what I mean."

"I think that's what I want, but — maybe that just sounds good for now. Maybe in a few years — oh, I don't know." She started to laugh. "Can you see me sitting up in one of those judge's chairs wearing a black gown and telling people they have twenty years in prison?"

"Black looks good on you. Makes your hair look sort of — "

"Oh, Cass!" She punched his arm.

"You know, Elizabeth, I really like you. A lot." He wasn't looking at her now. He was studying the empty street in front of him as if he was manoeuvring through a traffic jam.

"I know, Cass," she replied and snuggled against his arm, crushing the wilting corsage between them.

"Are you tired?" he asked against her forehead.

"No. Wired," she answered. "There's too much to think about." Being a judge. Going to university. Cass. And the persistent image of Woody telling her to be straight with her parents about everything.

"Yeah."

At first when they saw the police car parked just down the street they didn't think much of it. But Elizabeth quickly noticed that the front door of her house was wide open and that a police officer was standing inside.

"That cop car's in front of Woody's." Cass's voice had the same seed of panic that Elizabeth was feeling.

"It's Woody! Something's happened! Your bike's not back yet!"

"Maybe he's just still riding. He said he was having fun. He — "

But Elizabeth knew.

She ran up the pathway with Cass right behind her. "Mom! Dad! What's happened to Woody?"

Instantly her father was at the door, grabbing her and holding her like she was drowning. The police officer had his hat under his arm and he couldn't seem to look directly into anyone's eyes.

"Dad?"

But there wasn't any point in saying out loud what they all knew for sure. He just kept hugging her and trying to say something to Cass with his eyes. Cass reached out and touched Elizabeth's cast in a helpless gesture.

"Oh, no. Oh, no. Oh, no. Oh, no," Elizabeth repeated in a muffled moan into her father's chest.

"Your mother's over with Mrs. Harris," he said finally.

"I'm going over there!" Elizabeth didn't even know she was screaming. She ran out the door and down the sidewalk. Cass bolted after her. When he grabbed her she swung around fiercely as though she'd been captured. "Get your hands off me!"

"Stop it, Elizabeth!" He yelled so loudly his throat hurt, and he felt an insane urge to yell again.

They stood there facing each other, out of breath, stunned to silence.

Mr. Douglass and the police officer watched from the doorway as if they were afraid to move, afraid that, somehow, something else horrible might happen.

It seemed as if a long time passed. Nothing was real around them. There was no heat from the morning sun, no sense of the breeze touching their faces, no sound. Elizabeth's eyes were wide in fear.

Then she just seemed to lose all the tension that

had held her body stiff and all the fright that had flared in her eyes. She looked up at the leaves that rustled gently. Very softly, as if she were trying to change the meaning of her words, she said, "He's dead, Cass."

"Yeah," he whispered. He reached for Elizabeth's hand and took hold of the tips of her fingers.

"I loved Woody, Cass." Tears were beginning to slide down her cheeks again. "I love Woody."

Carefully, as if he might shatter her fragile calm, he took a step toward her and gathered her into his arms, tightly squeezing her as he too began to sob.

June 29

The day of Woody's funeral everyone came up to Elizabeth to give her a hug and to say they would miss Woody too. It seemed that most people were still in shock. It was as though Woody had taken off for a while but he'd be back before anyone had a chance to miss him for real.

There were a lot of things about Woody people wanted to talk about. Carolyn had taken two of the cotton candy cones from the graduation dance and she kept talking about when they'd made them. Belinda said she wished she could have gone to the graduation with him, or at least maybe just to a movie or something because he was such a nice guy. Sonia showed up and was crying so much her face was swollen and she kept asking Elizabeth if everyone was mad at her for leaving Woody at the dance. She must have asked that a hundred times. And Paul said that Woody was just about the best friend he'd ever had. He told Elizabeth about how Woody had promised never to tell that Cass had hit him that night in front of Frankie's. She figured it took a lot for Paul to admit that he'd been cleaned by Cass.

Mrs. Harris was a robot. Her husband led her around with his arm across her shoulders for support. She kept wanting to thank everyone for being friends with Woody.

She had developed the picture taken of Elizabeth and Woody on graduation night. Before the funeral she gave Elizabeth a copy. How could a few days seem like a million years? There they were, smiling into the camera. With her heels on, Elizabeth looked a lot taller than Woody. He was holding his shoulders back as if that would make up for being short. His bow tie practically screamed red. Mrs. Harris had managed to snap the picture without making the sunlight glint off his glasses and you could see the teasing look in his eyes.

Elizabeth had somehow done all right during the days before the funeral. Once she had finished crying, that panicky feeling that nothing could ever be normal again had subsided. She just felt numb.

The funeral was at eleven o'clock. At the back of the church a man stood pressing his hands together tightly as if he had something precious between his palms. A woman held his arm and gently rubbed her hand along the sleeve of his sports coat, as though that would ease the intense pain that showed in his eyes.

Elizabeth heard the man say, "I'm sorry," when Mr. Harris walked over to him but there was something different about the way he said it. Then it occurred to her. He must be the driver of the truck. Even though people were saying it was no one's fault, that man, she knew, would hold the horror in his mind forever. A million I'm sorries would not be enough.

The church was packed — students, friends, teachers, relatives, just everybody — and the altar was swamped with flowers. Elizabeth sat with Mr. and Mrs. Harris and Woody's grandparents. Mrs. Harris held her hand the whole time.

Yet in all that crowd, the church was empty, as empty as the most hollow space in the universe.

It was late in the afternoon before the Douglasses and Cass arrived back home.

There was nothing left to say.

"Dad, can Cass and I go for a drive?"

"Sure." He was doing what he could to make things better.

Her mother leaned to kiss her head and smooth her hair, the way she used to when Elizabeth was small.

"Where are we going?" asked Cass, adjusting the rear-view mirror.

"Back to the beach." Then, when he didn't say anything, she added, "I just want to be where we were all together last."

The tide had turned and the waves were beginning to climb back up the beach. No one else was there. The smooth sand was disturbed only by the tiny chiselled footprints of sandpipers and the webbed marks of gulls among the shattered clam shells.

Elizabeth walked a few steps ahead of Cass, listening to the waves and the breeze, and to her memory of what Woody had said that night.

"What are you thinking?" asked Cass.

"About Woody."

She saw him by the fire, sifting the sand back and forth in his hands. Then he was starting to say something about her and Cass but wouldn't finish.

A dozen or so sandpipers scattered as she and Cass approached them. The birds rushed on tiny legs, then flew up and settled a safe distance ahead.

Finally Cass and Elizabeth stopped where the charred stones of the graduation night bonfire formed a circle.

"I thought his footprints might still be here," said Elizabeth and she began to cry softly.

Cass kept hold of her hand but he didn't move.

"He shouldn't have died, Cass. He — he just — "

She tried to express her feelings but there were no words. She remembered sneaking out with Cass and panicking about Duncan and breaking her arm. Those things now seemed to be as insignificant as grains of sand.

"I wish it had been different when we were here," she said cautiously.

"Different? How?"

"Well, Woody and I had a fight when we were alone by the fire." It was a relief to say this out loud.

"Nothing seemed wrong to me."

"It wasn't really a fight. But I got peeved and — well — " She stared down at the cold, wet stones. "I figured we'd get a chance to straighten things out."

"Woody wouldn't have been really mad. What was it, about anyway?"

"About you and me partly."

Cass waited for her to continue.

"He stopped before he really said anything but I had a feeling about what he was going to say."

"So what was it?"

"He was trying to talk me into telling Mom and Dad about the accident and I was saying it was a waste of time to talk about something that was over since they were letting me go out with you now. Then he was about to say how you and I wouldn't last much longer."

Cass immediately remembered saying practically the same thing to Woody that night Woody had driven the bike for him, the night with the cops.

"What do you think, Cass? Was he right?"

The look in her eyes told him to hold back on any heavy thoughts for the moment. "I dunno. Who knows? All I can say is I want us to last."

"You said that your brother — "

"But he's not you. He never went with anyone in his whole life, so maybe university is different for him."

"I never wore your ring, Cass. Maybe I should wear your ring. That way people would know I was going steady."

"A ring won't keep guys away. Besides," he smiled weakly, "it won't fit." He slipped his large ring on her finger. "And it's heavy."

The gold-initialled ring hung loosely against her slim finger. Looking down at it, Elizabeth felt foolish. With a shove she forced it back over Cass's knuckle.

"I just don't want things to change."

Cass slid his hands around her waist and kissed her. "We've got a whole summer together before you go away." But how could he say more?

"It'll be so weird without Woody," she murmured against his shoulder.

"I think I'll give up smokes," Cass said finally, out of the blue.

"What?" Elizabeth wiped her wet eyes with her hand.

"I thought about it in church. I was watching Mrs. Harris and I was thinking about how she knows Woody's dead and she keeps wanting to talk about every little thing he did. I finally figured what that was all about. She doesn't want his past to die too. If no one remembers the details, then it would be like he never lived. Know what I mean?"

"Yeah. I think so."

"So I got thinking about that. Woody told me he quit smoking. I decided in church that I'd quit. At least for a while. Maybe for good."

"Oh, Cass." Tears blurred her eyes again. It was just that kind of dopey thing, she knew, that Woody would have really made fun of. He would like it but he would make fun of it until it drove you nuts.

She curled Cass's arm around her shoulder and made him hug her again. "I'm going to do something too."

"You don't need to do anything."

"Why?"

"You won't forget, that's why," he replied, kissing the end of her nose and smiling a crooked kind of serious smile.

Cass was right. She wouldn't forget. But Woody had been right too. She was sixteen and in a few months she'd be leaving home to go to university. If she didn't start playing straight with her parents now, it would be too late. Ancient history, like Woody had said that night. She wanted to finally explain the secret — all the secrets — to them. They'd given her a chance by letting her take Cass to the graduation. Now it was up to her to show them that she could handle things. She might still be their baby, but she wasn't a kid anymore.

"I think I'd like to go home now," she said.

Turning from the charred fire pit, they started back. Elizabeth began to think about how Mrs. Harris wanted to remember things about Woody's life. Maybe that really could kind of keep him alive in a hazy sort of way.

"Remember when Woody came to my birthday party without his glasses on?" she said, because that was the first detail that popped into her mind.

"He had them on when I saw him."

"Before that he didn't. There he was, as blind as a bat. And he was going to ask Belinda to graduation."

"Belinda?"

"Yeah. It was my idea. That was before Sonia asked him, when he didn't know who to take. Anyway, he had to keep asking where Belinda was because everything was a blur."